CORRUPTING CALI

SYNDICATE DADDIES
BOOK 1

KATE OLIVER

CONTENT WARNINGS

This book is a Daddy Dom romance. The MMC in this book is a Daddy Dom and the MFC identifies as a Little. This is an act of role-playing between the characters and falls under the BDSM umbrella. This is a consensual power exchange relationship between adults. In this story there are spankings and discussions of other forms of discipline.

This story is a big darker than some of Kate's other stories so if you prefer to avoid dark romance, this story may not be for you.

Please do not read this story if you find any of this to be disturbing or a trigger for you.

PROLOGUE

DECLAN

*S*ix *months ago…*

IT'S the one night a year I can go undetected. The one night I can walk into Surrender and nobody knows who the fuck I am. The crowd doesn't part as I walk through because they don't know the person under this mask is the head of the North American Irish Mafia. They're not afraid. Only Roman, the club owner, knows I'm here because I had to check in at the front desk when I came in, and he happened to be there.

My men keep a safe distance away, wearing their own costumes so they don't draw attention to me. I'm wearing a gray suit instead of my usual black. The full wolf mask and leather gloves with faux claws, hide my tattoos. I'm flying completely under the radar. It's a refreshing feeling but something that will only last for tonight. I can't walk around my city wearing a wolf mask all the time. Even if it is less scary to people than seeing my real face.

After getting a glass of whiskey from the bar, I head toward the only place I want to be for the rest of the night. A place where my darkness seems a little less ominous because of all the light that comes from the room. It's no place for a man like me. I'm dangerous. A fucking monster. But I can't help myself. It's what I like. It's the type of Dom that I am, and honestly, I can use all the light in my life I can get.

Opening the door, I look around and smile behind my mask. It's Halloween, and everyone is dressed up for the occasion. The club has a huge Halloween party each year, and everyone gets so damn excited for it since it gives them a reason to get all dressed up. The members go all out, and the owners give prizes for the best costumes.

I scan the room. I'm not sure what I'm looking for, but the behavior is ingrained after so many years. In my line of work, you must be aware of your surroundings. My men are always aware. It's how we've survived this long.

Princesses, pixies, angels, cowboys, and Prince Charmings are all over the room. Women and men dressed as adorable characters from their favorite movies. Two of my guys enter the room behind me, though they're still keeping their distance while two more stand in the hall keeping watch for any danger. My men and I share the same interests, so this room is like a candy store to us.

I've never hooked up with anyone at Surrender, but I think I come because this might be the closest I'll ever get to actually having a soft, submissive, and innocent woman in my life. I might be a monster, but I would never force a woman to become part of this life because of my own selfish needs.

Something red in the corner of the room catches my eye.

Red always catches my eye. It's the color of blood. It's probably fucked up to say it's my favorite color because of that, but you don't become the boss by being apologetic about who you are.

The woman in red is curled up on a huge bean bag with a book in her hand and a basket sitting next to her. It takes a moment for me to realize she's dressed as Little Red Riding Hood. And I'm the big, bad wolf. The air feels like it's sucked out of my lungs when I settle my gaze on her face.

Every once in a while, she looks up from her book and watches the crowd with a soft smile on her lips, and each time she does that, I get a glimpse of her big brown doe eyes. Her skin is milky, and her chestnut-colored hair is pulled into low pigtails that make her long tresses cascade down to her breasts.

Holy fuck, she's an angel. I've seen a lot of beautiful women in my life. I own dozens of strip clubs. I've seen the best of the best, but this woman tops them all by far.

Before I realize it, I'm making my way over to her, and though I have no fucking idea what I'm going to say, I know I have to talk to her. I need to hear her voice. I need to hear what she sounds like when she laughs. I need this more than I need air right now.

Coming to a stop in front of her, I stare at her for several seconds, frowning behind my mask at the fact that she's oblivious to me. Why isn't she paying closer attention to her surroundings? I instantly feel protective over her, and I also want to shake her a little and tell her she needs to pay better attention to who's approaching her.

As I clear my throat, she glances up and then does a double take. She can't see my face or any part of me behind my costume but I'm guessing the fact that she's Little Red and I'm the wolf is what's causing her to stare at me like she's seeing a ghost.

"Happy Halloween, Little Red."

A smile pulls at the corners of her mouth, causing her plump lips to look like a heart. It makes my cock thicken in my slacks.

"Happy Halloween, Wolf," she says softly.

Shit. Her voice sounds like an angel. She's beautiful. Even though she has some makeup on, I can tell she'd be just as gorgeous barefaced as she is tonight.

"No candy? Aren't Little girls like you supposed to be on a sugar high tonight?"

Her smile widens, and she reaches over to her basket and pulls a piece of cloth away to reveal a bunch of candy, making me chuckle.

"Hiding it, I see. That's kind of naughty."

Those brown eyes sparkle with mischief as she puts the cloth back in place, hiding her stash again. "I didn't want the wolf to come and steal it all. He's known for that, you know."

The grin I'm sporting behind my mask is so fucking wide, my cheeks are going to hurt in the morning. "Can I sit?"

She regards me for a second before she nods and moves her basket as if to keep it away from me.

Sitting on bean bags isn't exactly something I'm accustomed to, but for this girl, I'd sit on a bed of coals to talk to her for a few minutes. She's too sweet, too innocent, too everything I'm not for me to do anything more than talk to her, but I can't tear myself away.

Lowering myself to the beanbag, I lean my back against the wall and stretch my legs out in front of me. Getting this close to her was a mistake. I can smell her fragrance and it's making me feel drunk.

"What's your favorite kind of candy?" I ask, motioning toward her basket.

"Peanut butter cups. What's yours?"

"Snickers."

She grins and leans over to her basket. When she sits up

again, she holds out a miniature Snickers bar. "Since you're a nice wolf, I'll share."

I take the candy from her delicate fingers. "Just because the wolf seems nice doesn't mean he actually is."

She shrugs. "I have a feeling you won't hurt me, Wolf."

Fuck me. She's too damn sweet and innocent. I'd corrupt her whole world if she got involved with me. I can't do that to her. I don't have a lot of morals but for her, I have this one.

"What are you reading?" I ask, wanting to change the subject.

Her cheeks turn pink and her eyes lower to her book. "Uh, it's just a plain old boring romance book."

I wish she could see my face right now so she could see my raised eyebrow and stern expression over the fact that she just fed me a half-truth. It might be a romance book, but it's definitely not a plain old boring one based on the color of her cheeks.

Reaching out, I tug the book from her fingers and look at the cover. "*Haylee's Hero Daddy*. That seems like more than just a boring romance."

She reaches over and takes the book back, her cheeks a full-on scarlet color now.

"It's nothing to be ashamed of. We're here in this room. I assume you're a Little," I say.

"Maybe." She tucks the book under her thigh. "I'm not Little like some of them."

She's gesturing toward some of the women in the room who are obviously age players who play at a very young age. Some of them have pacifiers in their mouths. That's what this room was designed for.

It's almost as if she's ashamed she doesn't play that young, but I wouldn't care either way. I'm a Daddy Dom, through and through, but it's never mattered to me what age a woman plays at, as long as she's submissive, loves rough and dirty sex, and lets me take care of her.

"No? What's your Little like, then?"

She looks at me with wide eyes and thinks for a few seconds. "I'm not sure. I just, I like to feel young, I guess. I like being able to forget about my responsibilities and feel like someone else will take care of me. I like having my control stripped away so I can just relax and not have to think so much. Does that make me a fraud?"

I smile and shake my head. "No, baby girl. All of that makes perfect sense. You crave being looked after by someone who wants to care for you in a way that's more intimate than a vanilla relationship. You can still be Little without defining that side of you with a certain age. Some Littles fluctuate on age ranges they're most comfortable in, and sometimes it might change based on their mood. The most important thing about it is that you have a Daddy you can trust to take away all your choices so you don't have to think or worry about anything other than having fun doing whatever makes you happy. What do you like to do for fun when you're in this headspace?"

When she raises her big brown eyes to my mask, I can see the simple statement made her feel better, and the smile she gives me makes me so incredibly happy inside.

"I love puzzles and games. I like doing crafts too. I love to make bracelets and stuff like that. I always wanted one of those bracelet-making kits when I was a kid, but I never got one, so now whenever I can, I buy one and make them. I love to watch animated movies. Oh, and I love to paint and color."

Fuck, this Little girl is precious. The sad part is, I don't think she realizes it. "Those all sound like perfect activities for a Little girl like you."

She grins at me, obviously thrilled by my approval, and it makes me want to praise her even more.

"What's your name, Little Red?"

"Cali."

Nodding, I reach out my gloved hand to hers. "Nice to meet you, Cali."

She eyes my hand for a few seconds before she slides her smaller one into mine and shakes it. "Nice to meet you too, Wolf."

I need to get away from her. She's intoxicating, and if I don't get control of myself, I might do something stupid. As much as she'd be worth being stupid for, I won't drag her into my world. She's too fucking sweet and innocent. She's also everything I've ever dreamed of, and I know she'll be in my thoughts for the rest of my life. I'll probably hate myself for walking away, but it's for her own good. At least I'll keep telling myself that.

Getting to my feet, I look down at her one last time. "Be good, Red. Don't let any other wolves steal your candy."

The look of disappointment in her eyes almost kills me, but it's better this way. It's the only way I can make sure she's safe. She'll find a Daddy one day who won't have to walk away. The thought of her with another man wakes the monster inside me, but while I'm a selfish man, I can't be selfish with her.

"Goodbye, Cali."

I watch as she takes a sharp breath, pulling her bottom lip between her teeth, and then I force myself to turn and walk away. As I head toward the door, I hear her soft voice.

"Bye, Wolf."

My heart slams against my ribs, desperate for me to turn around. I force myself not to look back at her before I walk through the door and head toward the front of the club. Two of my men are in the hallway and instantly follow me after I storm past them.

"Find out everything about her. If she has a boyfriend, get rid of him. She's mine," I growl.

"Aye."

And with that, I burst out of the club and get into the waiting SUV, slamming the door behind me. "Go to the warehouse," I bark at my driver.

There's only one thing that will get my mind off Little Red Riding Hood, and unfortunately for the traitor being held at my destination, I'm feeling especially ruthless tonight.

1

CALI

P*resent day...*

"COME ON, Scarlet. The guy is a creep. Dump him. He's not Daddy material. He treats you like a possession."

This isn't the first time I've told my sister this. The guy she's dating has been being a jerk for months, and instead of leaving him like she should, she's been letting him treat her like shit.

It pisses me off to see my sister—who is also my very best friend—be treated like she's nothing. I hadn't liked the sound of the guy from the very first time she'd told me about him, but he'd treated her well in the beginning, so I had kept my mouth shut. But now, it's impossible to be quiet. She deserves so much better.

Scarlet shrugs and takes a sip of her energy drink before setting it on the counter where she'll surely leave it for days before she'll finally throw it away. "Cali, he's just stressed.

Work has been crazy for him and he's under a lot of pressure. You know he's about to become the boss."

I can't stop myself from rolling my eyes. "He's a gangster, Scar. I doubt that can be considered actual work. And if he can't handle the stress, maybe he shouldn't be the boss."

Her eyes widen. "You swore you'd never speak about it again."

I'd known the guy did some shady business from the get-go, but it wasn't until Scarlet and I got drunk off a cheap bottle of wine one night that she told me he was in the mob. Then she swore me to secrecy because she wasn't supposed to tell anyone. We never spoke about it again after that but it made me worry for her safety. Surely being the girlfriend of a mobster wasn't exactly safe. What do I know, though? I haven't had a boyfriend since high school, and my dating life in general is basically non-existent, so I really have no room to talk.

"Sorry. I just wish you would take a step back and really look at the way he treats you. He doesn't take care of you the way a Daddy should. He seems really selfish, and it's like you have to earn his attention and affection."

I hate ragging on my sister but she needs to hear it, even though I feel like an ass when her bottom lip starts trembling.

Bringing her hands up to her eyes, she wipes away the tears that start falling. "I just... I don't know if he'll let me break up with him, Cali."

My eyes widen because this is the first time she's ever said anything like this. "What do you mean, *let you*? He doesn't have to let you do anything. Just because you're Little doesn't mean you can't make your own choices."

Both my sister and I discovered we were Little when we were in high school. We're not sure if our fucked-up childhood is why we want a man who Daddies and dominates us, but whatever it is, it's something we both realized we wanted and needed when we were teenagers. She's actually had Daddies in real life—unlike me—but those so-called Daddies have all been crappy. I crave having a relationship like that one day in the future, just not with the type of assholes she's been with.

A flashback of a wolf fills my mind, and I force myself to push it away. It's been six months, and even though I've returned to Surrender dozens of times since that night, I've never run into him again. Not that I would know who he is because he had a mask on, but I was hoping he would see me and approach me. I really need to stop thinking about him.

Scarlet lets out a deep breath. "When we first got together, he said if I became his, I could never leave. Once you're attached to someone in the mob, you're attached forever."

I want to throw up. Surely the guy didn't mean it. He's just an emotionally abusive asshole. "Does he even seem like he wants to be with you?"

She shakes her head. "No. I'm pretty sure he's seeing someone else. I just…I'm afraid. Why do I always meet these men who claim to be Daddies but turn out to be assholes?"

I have an idea why, but I'm not about to say it out loud and make her feel worse than she already does. The thing about my sister is that she's so desperate for love and someone who cares for her that she doesn't look for red flags. She just dives right in head first and ends up getting burned. I love my sister with my whole heart, but I wish she would think things through a little more.

I wrap my arms around her tightly. "I don't know, sis. But you deserve better than him."

She hugs me back and nods. "I know. I'm going to tell him it's over. If he doesn't like it, well, too bad for him."

Even though I'm thrilled to hear she's going to end

things, a knot forms in my stomach. Hopefully Ivan doesn't act like a dick just because she doesn't want him. If the guy really is about to be a mob boss, he'll surely have women hanging all over him.

"I'm sorry I have to leave you feeling sad, but I have to go to work," I say as I let her go.

"I know. Sorry to cry on you. I'll be fine. I'm going to call him and break things off while you're gone, and tonight when you get home, we'll drink cheap wine and watch *Beauty and the Beast* while eating junk food."

A smile spreads across my face. "Sounds like a perfect night. I'll be home around eleven."

Scarlet nods. "I'll be waiting."

"I love you, Scar. It's going to be okay."

She flashes her gorgeous smile back at me. "I know. I love you, too. See you tonight."

WORK GOES WELL for the first few hours. Honestly, the past several months have been going very smoothly other than me worrying about my sister all the time. I don't know if I've done something at some point in my life that gave me some good karma, but my life has been going in the right direction for a change. Well, mostly. I've been on a couple of dates, only to have the guys ghost me after, but whatever. I wasn't really interested in them anyway. They never measured up to the wolf or the green-eyed god that I lay eyes on once a week at work. How pathetic am I that I'm hung up on a fictional character and a complete stranger?

I do get the occasional guy at the pub who creeps me out, and unfortunately I have one today. I didn't care for him the moment I greeted him, but I stay professional and ignore his innuendos. I pick up an order of drinks from the bar and smile as I make my way to the booth full of businessmen talking about whatever it is rich men like these talk about.

"All right, gentlemen, I have a round of bourbons," I say as I hand out their drinks.

They're all decently good looking, and since I started at this bar five months ago, they've been regulars of mine. They're kind and respectful to me, and they're good tippers. I have several groups that come in regularly and always tip well, actually. I feel really lucky to have gotten this job.

"Thanks, Cali," one of the men says.

Flashing them another smile, I head to my next table, stopping in my tracks when I see who the hostess just seated. I shouldn't be surprised. These six men come in every week, and they always sit in my section. They aren't just any men, though. I haven't figured out what they do for a living, but they look like they could be professional athletes. Tall, fit, dressed in expensive suits. These guys are by far my best tippers out of all of my regulars, and they always seem pleased to see me.

Even though they're all extremely handsome, one in particular makes my pussy wet, and I've spent some personal time with my vibrator while thinking about the guy. Thank goodness they tip so well because I swear, I have to buy new batteries on a weekly basis.

"Hey, lass," one of the men says.

All six of them have Irish accents, and it only adds to their hotness.

"Hi, gentlemen. Are you doing your usuals or something different today?" I ask as I look around the table.

My gaze stops on *him*. Just as it always does. He's sitting to my right, the same spot he always takes. His eyes get me every time. They're the clearest green I've ever seen. Not like a deep emerald green, either. They're more like a light sea-glass color. Clear, observant, sexy as hell. His eyes alone are enough to make me squirm.

"Same as always," he replies in a deep voice that causes a shiver to run through me.

I don't know his name. I've caught a few of the others — Killian, Ronan, and Bash — but no matter how hard I've tried, I've never heard his.

"I'll be right back." I make my way over to the bar, and before I even get there, the bartender is fixing their drinks.

As I watch the amber-colored liquid being poured from the bottle, I ponder my life and how things have changed so much lately. Six months ago, I was working at a different bar, one much less classy than O'Leary's Pub. I'd been on my eighth day straight of working at Pete's. I was exhausted and definitely not at my best when two men came in for drinks and food. At the end of their meal, one of the men introduced himself as Aiden O'Leary and offered me a job as a cocktail waitress at his pub for double what I was making at Pete's. I'd almost choked on my own spit. Aidan had said he liked how I worked and how the customers responded to me.

I took the job the next week and things have been going exceptionally well. I get to look at good-looking businessmen all the time, Aidan always schedules me to be in the VIP section so the tips are great, and he always gives me the most premium shifts. At first, I thought maybe he was doing all of those things because he was hoping to date me, but while he's friendly, he's never once acted in any way other than professional.

It's strange how one person can make such a substantial change in your life, but I'll always be thankful to Aidan for offering me the job.

The bartender snaps his fingers in front of my face. "Earth to Cali."

Looking up from the tray where I had zoned out, I smile at Liam. "Oh. Sorry. Daydreaming, I guess."

He gives me a knowing look, although what he knows, I'm not sure. I take the drinks over to the table and pass them out. When I first started working here, I thought maybe they were high-powered attorneys or something, but then I noticed the tattoos all over their hands and arms. Not exactly the look lawyers usually go for. Then I thought maybe they were soccer players. The Irish take their sports very seriously, and David Beckham has a million tattoos, so I thought maybe it was a soccer thing. But I'm pretty sure I'm wrong about them being professional athletes. So, I'm back to square one of not knowing what the hell these hotties do, and really, it's none of my business anyway.

"Are you hungry today or just having drinks?" I ask the table.

"Just drinks today, lass," the guy I'm pretty sure is Bash says.

All of these men are friendly and polite. But the one I want to hear talking the most is the quietest one. I can feel him watching me move around the pub whenever they're here. It's a strange feeling.

I'm not ugly, and my body is pretty tight for as little as I work out and as much as I eat, but I'm definitely not a beauty queen. I'm probably a solid seven out of ten on a good day. This guy is a one hundred out of ten. In other words, he's way out of my league. I have no idea why he watches me.

I leave their table and go check on my other customers, taking refills and food orders. Even though I'm in the VIP section, occasionally there's a customer who sits in my area and acts like an entitled asshole. Aidan has no tolerance for that kind of behavior from customers, so he's let me know I can kick anyone out who makes me feel uncomfortable. I've only had to do that once, and the guy was dragged out by a couple of the enormous security guards who are constantly on guard at the club.

I'm starting to think today might be the second time. This guy came in an hour and a half ago, and he's made sexual comments no less than a dozen times since then. As I walk up to his table, I hope he'll be ready for his check, but I can tell from the look in his eyes, leaving is the last thing on his mind.

"Can I get you anything else, sir?"

His eyes flash like a predator creeping up on a poor innocent bunny. "I like when you call me 'sir.' Maybe I'll take you to dinner sometime and you can call me that all night long."

I glance toward the front door where one of the security guards is scanning the pub. He makes eye contact with me as though he knew I was looking for him and then eyes my customer before giving me a sharp nod, letting me know he's on alert.

"Yeah, that is never going to happen. I'll just go get your check," I say.

As I turn to walk away, he grabs my wrist and yanks me so hard, I fall into his lap.

"Hey!" I cry out.

In a flash, I'm pulled up and set on my feet by one of the Irishmen. Not just any one of them, either. The one with the light-green eyes.

Bash is also there in an instant, guiding me away from the creep, but not before I see Mr. Green Eyes wrap his hand around the guy's throat, squeezing hard enough that he starts gasping for air.

"If you ever fucking lay a hand on her or any woman like that again, I'll kill you with my bare hands and then call your mother myself to come identify your corpse, you understand me?" he grounds out.

I'm too stunned to say or do anything. I couldn't if I wanted to because Bash is now standing in front of me with his arms behind his back holding me in place.

Everything is a blur, but then I see the creepy guy being carried out by the security guards and I feel like I can finally breathe a sigh of relief. The fact that I just saw Mr. Green

Eyes practically kill the guy with his bare hands right before my eyes doesn't scare me the way it probably should. For some reason, I feel safer.

He walks around Bash and looks down at me with a concerned expression. "Are you okay?"

I nod, biting my lower lip. "Yes. I'm good. Thank you."

When I look into his eyes, he's studying me so intently it makes a shiver run through my entire body.

"I'll fucking kill him," he murmurs as his gaze moves over my face.

My eyes widen, and I quickly shake my head. "I'm fine. I promise."

He studies me a bit longer with a look that almost seems a little sad. But then he backs away and nods at the other men with him. Everyone heads toward the door as he drops a wad of cash onto the table. Bash nods at me and offers a smile. "See ya later, lass."

I wave at him, but I'm still stunned over what happened. I glance at their table full of drinks that were hardly touched and then look at the cash. When I pick it up, my eyes widen. He left me a thousand-dollar tip. What the hell? They're always good tippers but never like this. I can't accept this.

Stuffing the cash into my apron pocket, I go back to work until Aiden comes in through the back door. He's usually only here in the evenings.

I make my way to his office and knock. He's frowning as he waves me in. "Hey, Cali. Are you okay? I got a message from James that some guy assaulted you, but he assured me it was handled."

I hold my hands up. "I'm fine. Really, I'm good. A customer came to my rescue and then James and Leon kicked him out."

Aidan stares at me for a long moment as if he's trying to figure out if I'm really okay. "Why don't you take the rest of the night off? I'll have someone drive you home."

My eyebrows pull together. "What? No. I'm fine. Really. I just came to talk to you because the customer who saved me, he uh, he left a really big tip, and I don't think I can accept it."

He leans back in his chair and smiles. "James told me Declan scared the piss out of the guy. Good for him. And if he gave you a big tip, it's because he thinks you deserve it, so of course you can accept it."

Declan. That was Mr. Green Eyes' name. It was just as sexy as the man.

"He left a thousand dollars," I blurt.

Aidan shrugs. "You deserve it, Cali. You work hard. You sure you don't want to take the rest of the night off?"

I sigh and nod, not saying anything else about the money because it's obvious Aidan won't let me give it back. "I'm good. Thanks, Aidan."

When I go back out, Sonya, another one of the cocktail servers, is standing near the bar. As soon as she sees me, she waves me over.

"Girl! What the hell? Liam told me Declan nearly killed a guy who put his hands on you," Sonya says a little more loudly than I'd like.

I put my index finger up to my lips, hoping she'll quiet down. "It was nothing. I'm fine."

Sonya flips her ponytail over her shoulder and raises her eyebrows. "I don't know if I'd be fine knowing a mob boss was ready to kill someone for me. Pretty sure I'd come in my panties."

I want to laugh at the last part but my heart is too busy racing at the first part. "What do you mean *mob boss*?"

She tilts her head and glances back at Liam, who shrugs and doesn't say anything. "Declan Gilroy is the leader of the Irish Mafia here in the States. He owns, like, all of Seattle and most of the West Coast. He's the most powerful man in this area. How did you not know that?"

Without saying anything, I walk away. I head for the bathroom because suddenly, everything seems to hit me at once, and instead of being shaken up or upset, I'm so unbelievably turned on. What the hell is wrong with me? I need therapy. Serious fucking therapy.

2

DECLAN

He fucking *touched* her. Killian follows me into the waiting SUV while my other men get into the car behind us. My driver immediately takes off for my estate while I'm looking for something to punch. I have half a mind to track the fucker down and kill him like I so badly want to.

Killian says nothing because he knows I need a minute to calm down. I'm not usually hot-headed. Only when it comes to her. I grab hold of the Jameson bottle that's stored in the door.

"If you're going to smash that, can I get out of the car first?" Killian asks.

I give him the finger as I pull off the cap and take a hefty pull directly from the bottle. "Fuck off," I say as I hold it out for him to take.

Killian is my best friend. He's also my right-hand man. I trust him as much as I trust my brothers, and that's saying something. Trust doesn't come easily when you're in the mafia. It's something that has to be earned. Killian has earned it time and time again.

"I want more security at her apartment complex," I say.

He wipes his mouth with the back of his hand and chuckles. "If we put any more security in her apartment building, she's going to feel like she's living in a penitentiary."

It's true. In the past six months, I've had cameras, automatic door locks, and fingerprint readers installed in the elevators. I also had a desk with twenty-four-hour trained security guards put in the lobby. There is no such thing as going too far when it comes to her safety.

Yeah, I'm obsessed. I have been since the night I met her. I've done everything in my power to make her life better, and I'd like to think I've taken care of her in the only way I can. From a distance. Because she is too sweet and too pure for me to pull her into my darkness. The risk it would put her at is too great.

I can't keep scaring away her dates forever. It isn't fair to her. She deserves to be happy and to find a Daddy who will take care of her. No one will ever be able to take care of her the way I can, but they won't put her in danger either. Maybe someday I'll approve of one of her dates, but I'm not ready to let go of her yet. I don't have the strength. As selfish as it is, I consider her mine.

"Why don't you just take a chance with her, D?"

Killian is the only person in the world with the balls to call me D. I hate it and he knows it, but he continues to call me that whenever he wants to irritate me.

"We've talked about this before. This life isn't for her. And who knows if she'd even be interested in me."

My best friend smirks. "Ever think maybe you should let *her* decide if this life is for her? I see the way she looks at you. She's fucking into you. Any idiot can see that."

I glare at him. "It's not her decision to make. It's mine." I snatch the bottle back from his grasp and take another long pull, letting the liquid warm me on the inside.

"Aye, Boss."

That's Killian's way of agreeing with me even though he

doesn't really agree with me. That's the problem with having your best friend as your right hand. He might be calling me boss, but I know he's really calling me dumbass in his mind. Fucker.

I NEED TO BE WORKING, but it's after eleven, and all I can do is stare at the large monitor mounted on a wall in my office and watch the surveillance of Cali's apartment as I wait for her to get home. I do this every night she works. It doesn't matter that I have two of my men tail her from the pub to her apartment complex. Until I see her walk into her apartment, I can't relax.

Even though I have work that needs to be done, I ignore it as I lift my glass to my lips and take a swig of whiskey. Work can wait. Her safety is more important. I know her work schedule because Aiden sends it to me every week. Even though he "owns" O'Leary's, technically the pub belongs to the mob, and Aiden is one of my men. He also helps manage several of the other pubs we own while funneling cash through them at the same time.

It wasn't a coincidence that Aiden found Cali and offered her a job. When my men told me where she worked, I nearly lost it. Pete's is known for its rowdy crowd and college-aged kids partying there every weekend. The thought of some college punk looking at her ass or hitting on her had been enough for me to see red, so I had Aiden go there and offer her a job. Thank fuck she took it because if she hadn't, I probably would have gone all caveman and dragged her out of there myself.

In the past six months, I've learned everything I can about Cali Jenkins. She's twenty-four, making her twenty-two years younger than me. She grew up just outside of Seattle and lives with her sister, who is two years younger.

Her sister is much more social than Cali from what I can tell. While I rarely see Cali leaving her apartment other than to go to work, Scarlet goes out frequently, though I have no idea where she goes because I don't follow her like I follow Cali. The two women grew up without a dad and their mom has been in and out of rehab multiple times throughout the years with several arrest records for drug possession. From what I can tell, Cali and Scarlet raised themselves. They don't have any other family in the area, and based on their phone records, they never talk to their mom who now lives in Oregon.

My men keep me informed of anything they think I need to know. Like the times Cali has gone out on dates. After those dates, my men tracked down the jackasses and paid them to stay the fuck away from her with the lingering threat that if they didn't, they would be sorry.

Given that the men had happily taken the money and never contacted her again, I knew they weren't anywhere near good enough for her anyway. She deserves someone who will fight for her. Not that I have any goddamn room to talk. All I'm doing is watching her and trying to make her life easier. She's worked too hard for too long, and she deserves to live easily. It's the least I can do since I can't actually make her mine.

Movement on the screen brings me back to reality. She enters the lobby and greets the night guard before taking the elevator up to her floor. I hate that I'm not with her, leading her home to tuck her into bed and cuddle her to sleep. I hate that she goes to bed alone each night, and I wonder if she ever thinks of me as she touches herself like I think of her when I jerk off.

As soon as I see her door close, I take a deep breath and lean back in my chair, resting my head against soft leather. There are so many things I wish I could change about this situation, but unfortunately, being in the mob isn't something I can quit. Once you're in, it's for life. There is no out.

I think about the way that motherfucker grabbed her earlier in the day and my hands tighten around my glass. I should have killed him for daring to touch her. I don't tolerate abusing, selling, or hurting women. All of my men feel the same, and anyone under my command who's crossed those lines is no longer living. It's been that way forever. My father had the same rules about women. We protect them. Never harm them. Which is why keeping her at a distance is the best for her because if I bring her into my world, I can't guarantee her safety no matter how many guards I have.

The way she reacted to the guy hitting on her was impressive. It didn't seem to faze her, and she didn't back down. She also didn't scream or freak out when she saw me nearly snap his neck. It makes me wonder if she's been around violence before. Then again, she did work at Pete's, so I'm sure she's had to tell guys to fuck off more than once. That thought pisses me off again. I slam my drink down on my desk and decide to call it a night before I start looking for any man who has ever disrespected or hurt her.

3

CALI

It's still so weird walking into my apartment building and seeing a security guard. Over the last several months, the building has installed all kinds of security. I was happy when it first started happening, but then Scarlet and I panicked because while we do okay financially, we definitely can't afford for the rent to increase. I called the management office and they assured me they wouldn't be increasing our rent one bit.

"Hi, Henry," I say as I walk through the lobby.

"Good evening, Miss Jenkins. Have a good night."

I smile at him as the elevator doors close me in, and I press my fingerprint against the reader that allows me to get up to my floor. Scarlet is waiting for me in the living room when I walk in. She already has a glass of wine in her hand, and the bottle and an empty glass are sitting on the coffee table. I grin. "Getting a head start?"

She snorts and holds her glass up. "Yes. You took too long. I needed a drink."

Giggling, I plop down on the couch beside her and rest my head on her shoulder. "Sorry. I'll go change and then we can start our girls' night and you can tell me how it went with Ivan."

I hop up from the couch, go into my room, and strip out of my dress. I have five dresses I rotate wearing for work. They're all fitted and land mid-thigh. A couple of them are long sleeved for when the weather is cooler, and they're each a different color. Aiden gave me a clothing allowance when I first started and told me dresses were the uniform but it was up to me what kind I chose. I looked at what the other cocktail servers wore and based my choices off of that. If I'd bought what I liked, I would have chosen baby doll dresses or something similar that was more comfortable.

I find my favorite pair of pajamas—a pair of pink cotton shorts and a matching pink tank top that have bunnies printed all over them. They're cute and they make me feel a little less adultish, if that's even a thing. I like cutesy stuff like that. And anything pink.

My sister is in the kitchen, pulling a bag of Cheetos from the cabinet, when I return to the living room. I pour myself a hefty glass of wine and sit cross-legged on the couch. She's already crunching on the cheese-flavored snack when she sits back down.

"Cheetos?" she asks, holding out the bag.

This is what our girls' nights usually look like. Wine, Cheetos, and *Beauty and the Beast* or some other animated movie. We keep it classy. Obviously.

"Duh. Is that even a question?" I ask.

I grab the bag from her hand and start eating while looking at her expectantly. I want to know what happened between her and Ivan. My mind flashes to Declan and I wonder if the two men know each other. I'm pretty sure Scarlet said Ivan was in the Russian mob, so does that mean the men would be enemies? I have no idea how all this gangster stuff works. Quite frankly, I prefer to be ignorant to that kind of stuff. I had enough drama in my life when I was growing up. I try to keep things as low-key as possible now.

"Are you going to tell me what happened or do I have to stare at you all night, waiting?" I finally ask.

My sister laughs and rolls her eyes as she takes a drink of her wine. Then she shrugs and bites her bottom lip, a hint of sadness in her eyes. "He told me I'd be sorry for leaving a man like him. He said some other mean things and called me names and then told me it was my loss before he hung up. It kind of hurt that he didn't even seem to care, but at the same time, I'm relieved he didn't totally freak out or something. I know it's for the best, but I just wish someone would fight for me for once, you know?"

I do know. Neither of us have ever had anyone fight for us. I reach for her hand and squeeze it. "When the right one comes along, he'll fight for you."

She sniffs and nods. "I know."

The memory of Declan threatening to kill the creep who grabbed me comes to mind, causing a shiver to run through me from head to toe. Knowing he's in the mafia, it doesn't seem strange that he would choke someone in the middle of a restaurant, but what I find strange is why he felt the need to protect *me*? I'm nobody to him.

Whatever the reason, heat spreads through me, and I find myself shifting into a position where I can squeeze my thighs together because my pussy is suddenly throbbing.

"Come on. It's time to get drunk and watch our favorite movie. Fuck Ivan," Scarlet says with a grin.

I smile back and hold up my glass. "Fuck Ivan. Cheers!"

I CAN'T STOP THINKING about Declan. The way his eyes follow me when he's at the pub. The way he protected me from that asshole. The way his tattoos cover the backs of his big hands. I wonder how those hands would feel on my body. On my breasts. My clit. Wrapped around my throat. Those hands could easily turn my bottom red, and that thought makes me squirm.

It's been too long since I've been spanked. The last time was over a year ago at Surrender. A Daddy Dom had seen me watching someone get spanked, and when he'd noticed how intrigued I was, he'd offered to turn my bottom red and hot. I've always been the good girl, the rule follower, the one who is much too serious for her age. When he'd offered, I almost said no, but something inside of me had told me I needed it. I needed the release of a spanking that I'd heard and read about. The man was kind and controlled and handsome, though I wasn't attracted to him. One of the club monitors vouched for him, so I'd let him spank me, and that spanking had awakened something inside of me I never knew I needed. Now it's something I crave. It was the closest thing to a sexual experience with a man I've ever had. Why can't a man like Declan go to Surrender? Because the only man I can imagine spanking me now is him.

A tray of drinks being set down in front of me brings me back to reality, and I smile at the bartender as I pick up the tray to deliver to a table. It's almost the end of my shift, and I'm ready to go home and drink cheap wine with Scarlet. It's been three days since she broke up with her shitty ex and we've been celebrating with cheap wine and Cheetos every night since. She's happier without him, and I feel like I don't have to worry about her so much.

After delivering the drinks, I start cashing out my credit card tips. Aidan walks up and smiles down at me. He's been checking on me every day since the incident with the creep to make sure I'm okay. I keep telling him I'm fine, but he's like an overprotective uncle or something.

"I'm fine, Aidan," I say before he even asks.

He grins and winks at me. "Of course you are. You're a tough one. I knew it when I hired you."

I roll my eyes because he's totally blowing smoke up my ass, but at the same time, I appreciate his compliment. "Thanks."

"Get out of here. I'll have one of the late-shift waitresses finish up your last table."

Normally, I'd insist on finishing out my shift, but for some reason, I decide to take him up on his offer. I want to get home, put on a pair of my cutest pajamas, and hang out with my best friend in the whole wide world while eating junk food.

"If you're sure?"

He nods. "I'm positive. Go. I'll see you tomorrow."

Within ten minutes, I'm on my way home. While stopped at a light, my phone chimes with the sound I've assigned only to my sister. She's probably calling me to tell me to stop and pick up more wine. Smiling to myself, I grab my phone and answer it.

"Hey, Scar, what's up?"

All I can hear on the other end is her crying and some muffled male voices with a strong accent. My blood runs cold.

"Scarlet? Can you hear me?"

"Let me go!" she screams.

I hear the deep laughs of men in the background.

"You should have known not to fuck with the boss," one of the men says in a thick Russian accent.

My entire body starts shaking as I call her name again before I hear more muffled cries and then a loud crashing sound before the line goes dead.

"Scarlet!" I scream.

A horn blares behind me. The light is green. I step on the gas and start driving, though my entire body is shaking. What was that crashing sound? It sounded like her phone hit something. Did they throw it on the ground? Where is she? Were those men in my apartment?

So many possible scenarios run through my mind, and with each passing second, I'm imagining more horrible things than the last.

Her car isn't in the garage when I park, and I rush inside the building. With barely a glance at the guard, I make a beeline for the elevator. My hands tremble. I can barely get my finger on the scanner. It takes forever to reach the ninth floor.

When I get to my door, it's locked, and I can't hear any noise inside, so I fumble to get my key into the slot. I prepare for the worst, but everything looks just like it had when I'd left for work earlier in the day. I close the door behind me and run to Scarlet's room, but it's empty and nothing looks out of place.

I move through the apartment, hoping Scarlet is hiding in a closet or under one of our beds, but once I've looked in every nook and cranny of the space, I come to the cold hard conclusion that she isn't here, and suddenly I crack. My knees give out, and I drop to the floor, letting out deep sobs.

The mob has my sister. That bastard has my sister. What do I do? Should I call the police? Will it even make a difference? It's not like this guy is some street criminal. He's the goddamn mafia. They're untouchable, right?

Sobs continue to rack my body. They're going to kill her. I know it. I knew he was dangerous. I should have known he wouldn't let her break up with him so easily. She hurt his ego, and in return, he's going to kill her.

I don't know how long I sit on the floor and cry but the tears just keep coming, and when I'm so weak I can barely even stay sitting up, I lower myself to lie on the floor and cry some more until eventually my exhaustion becomes so heavy, I can't keep my eyes open.

4

DECLAN

I don't want to be here. It's past eleven at night on the West Coast and here I am in fucking Chicago to meet with the heads of the various crime families. It's been nearly a year since we all met and I could have gone another year if it were up to me. But Vladimir Petrov, the head of the Russian syndicate, has called a meeting, so here the fuck I am.

I hate that I'm not watching my surveillance to make sure Cali makes it home okay. Even though I know my men will tail her all the way to her apartment and her entire building is secure now, I still like to see her to her door every night, even if it is through a screen.

Killian is standing behind me while I'm sitting at a large boardroom table. All the leaders and their seconds in command are here. The Italians, the Russians, the Cartel, the Albanians, the Chinese, the Serbians, and every other family who has their syndicate touching American soil.

For the past thirty years, there's been a pact in place for no bloodshed or war. Everyone has respected that pact. It's been good for all of us. We respect each other's territories, and any time any of us have found a traitor in our ranks, it's dealt with swiftly.

Despite the pact, I don't trust most of the men around this table. Alessandro De Luca, head of the Italian syndicate, is the only man here I can confidently say I trust. He and I grew up knowing each other. His father was the head of the Italian Mafia at the same time as my father headed our mafia. The two were friends, and Alessandro and I have known each other long enough that we have a mutual respect for one another. I know if I ever needed help from another syndicate, he would be there, just as I would be for him.

I'm getting agitated that this meeting hasn't started yet. The sooner it starts, the sooner I can get the fuck out of Chicago and back to Seattle. For some reason, Vladimir is stalling and it's pissing me off.

Suddenly, the door opens and a younger man walks in. Vladimir's son. I don't like the kid. I met him a few times while he was growing up and I've known since he was young that he had an ego the size of Texas. While having a big ego in this line of work is necessary, you also have to keep it in check. I don't think he's the kind of man to keep it in check.

Alessandro and I glance at each other and I can sense his unease as well. Whatever this meeting is about, I have a feeling it's not going to be good.

"Gentlemen, thank you for joining me tonight," Vladimir finally says in his thick Russian accent.

Everyone's attention turns to the older man, and I sit back in my chair and wait to hear whatever it is he has to say. I can feel Killian's tension behind me. He feels the same way about Vladimir and his son as I do.

"As you all know, I've been having some, eh, health troubles," Vladimir says.

Yeah, no shit. The fucker is like three hundred pounds and eats Russian Napoleon Cake like it's a salad. He also drinks like a fish, and I've never seen the guy without a cigar in his hand. I'm all about enjoying your life, but in moderation.

"It is time for me to retire as boss," Vladimir says before taking a puff from the cigar resting between his sausage fingers. "I'm naming my son, Ivan Petrov, as the head of the Russian syndicate. I'll be staying on as his advisor as he transitions into the role."

The room is dead silent as we take in this information. All of the men here have learned to never react to anything too quickly as it can make you seem weak. On the inside, I'm livid. It should be Vladimir's right-hand man stepping into the role as boss, not some twenty-something-year-old kid who hasn't worked his way through the ranks.

I glance at Ivan's face, which is a mistake because it makes me even more pissed. The kid looks like a snake that's just found its first big meal in a long time. This is going to be a fucking mess. There is nothing on this kid's face that tells me he will respect the other syndicates. He's the type of guy who wants as much power as he can get, and he will do whatever it takes to get it. This is something that won't end well for him, but it could cause a lot of problems in the meantime. I don't have time for problems. I'm running a successful operation while making myself and my men rich, and the violence between syndicates has been non-existent. I'd like to keep it that way. I know my men would too.

Vladimir blathers on, assuring us everything will remain the same among us, it will be an easy transition, and the pact will still be honored. All while his snake of a son is standing behind him with a puffed up chest like he's king of the world. It will be fun to watch him lead his way into his own doom.

It's after one in the morning by the time the meeting adjourns. I walk out with Killian by my side and four of my men flanking me. None of the bodyguards go into the meeting room. Only bosses and underbosses. That way if anyone decides to pull a gun or let their emotions get the best of them, it's all on them and not their bodyguards.

The six of us are silent as we make our way toward the SUVs. Alessandro will want to discuss this, but we ignore each other as we get into our separate cars. This will be a conversation had in private over the phone so as not to show our personal alliance to the other leaders. Better to keep things like that a secret.

As soon as the car door closes and Killian and I are alone, he curses.

"This is going to be a fucking disaster. That kid has no intention of keeping our pact. As soon as power is turned over, everything will go to shit."

All I can do is nod because Killian is spot on. "Aye."

I pull my phone out of my pocket and look at my text messages, opening the one from my men who secretly escort Cali home each night. The message confirms they followed her home and that they saw her enter the apartment complex. It soothes my nerves a bit, but I still take the glass of whiskey Killian hands me because fuck, this night was shit.

THE NEXT MORNING, I'm in the middle of briefing my closest men about the situation with the Russians when my phone rings and I see Aiden's name showing on the caller ID. He rarely calls me unless it has to do with Cali, so I snatch my phone from the table and answer it, my men going silent around me.

"Yeah?"

"Hey. Just letting you know Cali is out sick today."

I sit up straighter, feeling my back go rigid. "What kind of sick?"

The fact that she's at home, sick, with no one to take care

of her makes me feel like shit. I should be there. But I can't just storm the place and take over. Well, I could. I'm a fucking mob boss, I can do whatever I want. But I also suspect she wouldn't be very welcoming toward me if I did.

"I'm not sure. She texted me a few minutes ago and said she wasn't feeling well and she needed to stay home today."

"Did she seem like she didn't feel well last night?" I ask.

Aiden would have called me if she'd been sick last night. He's been instructed to call me with any little thing he notices about her. So much as a cough or tear and I expect a phone call, but I still have to ask.

"No, she seemed fine. I let her leave an hour early because it was slow, but she seemed like her normal self."

Shit. I don't like this. I have no way to check on her. The only place she has any privacy from me is inside the walls of her apartment. I have eyes on her everywhere else. A thought occurs to me and I look to Grady, one of my men sitting at the table. "Is her sister home?"

Grady shakes his head. "She left last night around nine and hasn't come home yet."

That wasn't totally out of the ordinary.

"Call me if you get any updates from her, and I want to know if she's back at work tomorrow. I'll be stopping by to check on her if she is."

"Aye, Boss," Aiden says before ending the call.

The rest of my day is shot because I'm going to be worrying about my Little girl until I know she's okay. I should be there with her. I fucking hate having to take care of her from a distance. Moments like this make me wonder if it really is better to stay away. She needs to be held and taken care of if she's not feeling well. I need to be there holding her.

My brother Sebastian—Bash for short—is already tapping away at his phone.

"I'm sending a wrong address delivery to her. We'll at

least be able to find out if she's really sick, and if so, how bad," Bash says.

I really love my brother sometimes. He's a smart ass and stubborn as fuck, but he knows I care for her so he does too. All of my guys do. Even if they think I'm an idiot for not making her mine. They don't say it. They just help me take care of her because if she's important to me, she's important to them.

5

CALI

I didn't realize it was possible for someone to cry so much, but when I woke up in the middle of the night while still on the floor, my tears started all over again, and they haven't stopped since. I couldn't get myself under control enough to go to work, so I called in sick for the first time since I started at the pub.

Eventually I called the police even though I knew they wouldn't be much help, and I was right. Since Scarlet hasn't been missing for forty-eight hours, they wouldn't even file a missing person report. That just caused me to cry even more until I fell asleep again on the couch.

Later that evening when someone knocked at my door, I practically ran to answer it, hoping to find my sister on the other side, but it was just a delivery of flowers to the wrong address. The delivery guy took one look at me and asked if I was okay. When I told him I was fine and just a little under the weather, he'd eyed me with a frown before he left to make the delivery to the correct apartment. Then I cried myself to sleep but tossed and turned all through the night.

Today I've forced myself to take a shower and pull myself together for work. I have no idea what to do or how to start looking for my sister, but I still have to work. If anything, I'm hoping it will take my mind off things for a few hours, but first I have to force myself to get out of my car and go inside.

I have about half a tube of concealer under my eyes, and I can still see how puffy they are when I look in the mirror. No matter how much ice, concealer, or eye cream I used, nothing helped. Sniffling again, I close my eyes and say a silent prayer for my sister before I finally get out of my car. My entire body aches with each step, and I can feel the security guards' eyes on me as I enter the pub. I offer them a weak smile and avoid eye contact, thankful they don't ask me any questions as I pass by.

As soon as I clock in, I start taking tables in an attempt to keep myself busy and avoid conversation with my coworkers.

Not even twenty minutes go by before I see Declan and his friends enter and head straight toward their table. All six men watch me with concerned expressions. As soon as I meet Declan's gaze, his eyebrows furrow, and I look away as I force a smile to the rest of them.

"Hi, gentlemen. Your usual drinks?" I ask with enthusiasm I don't feel. Even I can hear how fake I sound.

"Aye, lass. Are you doing okay?" one of them asks.

I think his name is Killian, but I'm too exhausted and emotionally spent to keep track of who's who at the table.

"I'm good, thanks," I lie. "I'll be right back with your drinks."

Declan says nothing but as I walk away, I swear I can feel his searing gaze at my back. If I weren't so upset, I'd probably be turned on by the fact that he watches me so closely. It feels intimate in a way I can't explain.

Liam eyes me while he pours the drink order. "You okay, Cali?"

"What? Oh, uh, yeah." I wave my hand in the air nonchalantly.

I'm so not okay. But talking to my coworkers about this isn't something I want to do. They can't help me anyway. No one can help me. The cops won't take a report until tomorrow, and I don't have much confidence that they'll be able to help. I need someone powerful enough and knowledgeable enough about how the mob works.

I glance over at the table of Irishmen and notice several of them looking at me, including Declan. The head of the Irish Mafia.

Sonya's words play in my mind. *He's the most powerful man around here.*

Before I realize what I'm doing, I'm beelining toward their table, my eyes focused on Declan. "Can I speak with you?" I blurt out.

All it takes is a single nod of his head and the other five enormous men rise from their chairs and disappear without a word.

"Have a seat, Cali," he says, motioning to the chair next to him.

I sit. I'm on the edge of falling apart again but I force myself to swallow the lump forming in my throat. His green eyes are focused on me and even though his expression is confident and stern, I can also see worry in his gaze.

"What's wrong, Little girl?" he finally asks when I don't say anything.

His endearment makes me pause. I let it soak in. It's a strange feeling. I feel comforted in a way.

"I, uh, I heard you're a mafia boss, and I don't know what else to do or who to go to. I need help. My sister," I say, a sob catching in my throat.

He turns his entire body toward me, his eyebrows furrowed with concern. "What happened, baby?"

I'm too busy trying not to totally lose it to fully register him calling me baby. "She's been kidnapped. By...by..."

I can't hold it together anymore, and before I realize it,

Declan is lifting me from the chair and carrying me toward the back of the club, right into Aiden's empty office. He kicks the door closed behind us and sets me down on the couch, kneeling on the floor in front of me. His enormous body fills the space. Even though I've never seen him without his suit jacket, I can tell he's muscular under the perfectly fitted fabric. His eyes seem darker than usual as he stares at me and his jaw is tense. I can't look away from his gaze, and I don't want to, either.

"Who was she kidnapped by, Cali? What happened? Tell me." His voice is firm but soothing. My breath saws in and out of my lungs, and it feels like my chest is burning.

Declan's warm hand reaches out and grips my chin, forcing me to look at him. "Cali, breathe. One breath in, then out."

I obey without thinking and start to calm.

"Good girl." His warm hand is still holding my chin, and the sensation helps to soothe me even more.

When I feel like I can finally breathe normally again, I offer a weak smile. "I'm sorry."

He shakes his head. "No need to be sorry, baby. Just tell me what happened."

I nod and sniffle as I wipe the tears falling down my cheeks. "My sister—her name is Scarlet—she was dating a guy in the mob. He wasn't nice to her, and she finally broke up with him. Everything was fine, but two nights ago, on my way home from work, she called me. She was begging someone to let her go and there were men in the background laughing and saying she shouldn't have broken up with him, and then I think they got her phone and smashed it or something because the line went dead."

As soon as I finish, a sob breaks free and my tears start again. Declan has his arms wrapped around me in an instant, and I find myself burrowing my face into his chest, crying almost hysterically.

"Shh. I've got you, Little one. It's going to be okay."

I know he's only saying these things to make me feel better, but for some reason, I believe his words. Maybe I'm just grasping for some kind of hope to hold onto but whatever it is, it's helping.

"S-she's m-my best fr-friend," I cry.

He strokes the back of my head, and I continue to cry, soaking his suit jacket with my tears. "Cali, look at me."

I pull back and gaze at his handsome face. Even though I know he's the leader of a criminal organization, I feel safe.

"Good girl," he says, brushing some of my stray hairs away from my face. "What mob, baby? Does this guy know where you live?"

I nod and hiccup. "Yeah, he was there once to pick her up. He's...he's Russian, I think."

I'm surprised when Declan lets out a string of curse words. He pulls out his phone.

"Bring a car around back. I'm bringing her out. Call a meeting."

He slides his phone back into his suit pocket. "We need to go. If this guy is in the mob, he might come after you too."

Before I get the chance to say anything, Declan picks me up from the couch. Panic rises in my chest again. Where is he taking me?

"Wait. I have to work. I can't leave," I tell him.

Not that I'm in any shape to keep working. I'm a mess, and I'm sure I have makeup smeared all over my face. If Declan weren't dressed in all black, he would probably have noticeable mascara smears all over his shirt.

"You can't stay here. It's not safe."

Suddenly I realize I have no idea what I've just gotten myself into. This man—who I know is a criminal—is trying to leave with me, and I have no idea if I can actually trust him. What if he's friends with Ivan and turns me over to him?

I start to struggle in Declan's arms. "I can't leave. I'll get fired. Please, put me down."

He must hear the panic in my voice because he sets me down on the couch again and makes another call. "I need you in your office. Now."

Within seconds, Aiden walks in, looking concerned. "Hey, boss. What's wrong?"

I look between the two men in complete confusion. Boss?

"Until further notice, Cali is on leave from work. If anyone comes here looking for her, I need to know, ASAP."

Aiden nods. "Of course, boss."

Declan looks down at me. "Aiden works for me. The pub belongs to us. He can vouch that you'll be safe with me. We don't harm women. I can protect you, but I need you to let me. I can also try to find out what happened to your sister. I would never hurt you, Little one."

I'm so incredibly confused.

Aiden squats down in front of me and looks at me as if I'm a child with a scraped knee. "You're safe with him, Cali. I promise. Whatever's going on, let him help you. You'll continue to get paid, and your job is safe here when you return."

Tears slip down my cheeks as I nod and wipe them away with the backs of my shaking hands. Declan's gaze hasn't left my face the entire time Aiden's been in the office, and I realize he's my only option for help. If he decides to hurt me or give me to Ivan, that's a chance I'm willing to take. I have no other way to find my sister, and I feel completely defeated. I'm so tired I can't rationalize anything. I went to him for help, and I need any help he can give me.

Dropping my shoulders, I nod. "Okay."

6

DECLAN

I'm seething inside. I want to break everything in this fucking office. I can't stand seeing Cali like this. Her skin is paler than I've ever seen it. She has dark circles under her eyes. I have a feeling she hasn't eaten since her sister disappeared, and she's barely coherent.

I know it's not anyone within my organization because if any of my men ever kidnapped a woman, I would have their heads. Cali is too distraught right now for me to ask her a bunch of questions, and I need to get her out of this pub and to the safety of my house. If these fuckers came for her sister, there's always a chance they might come for her too, and that isn't something I'll ever allow.

I take Cali's hand gently and lead her out of the back of the pub where my men are waiting. She's shaking so badly I have to wrap my arm around her waist to keep her steady.

"I need my purse," she says suddenly.

Without a word, Bash goes inside and reappears a moment later with her purse, handing it to her. I grab hold of her waist and lift her into the SUV. My driver, Connor, is already behind the wheel, ready to take off at a moment's notice if needed. Before I close the door, I reach in and grab the seatbelt to fasten her safely inside. She offers me a weak smile, and I can't resist lifting my hand to her face to wipe the tears from her cheeks with my thumb.

"It's going to be okay, baby girl," I tell her.

The look on her face tells me she isn't so sure. I don't know what the outcome of all of this will be, but I will make sure my baby girl is okay. I hope to God her sister is still alive and we can find her before whoever took her decides on her expiration date.

After I close her into the SUV, I look at my guys, who are all waiting to hear what's going on.

"Her sister was kidnapped. Cali says it was someone from the mob, and she thinks he's Russian. That's all I know. I'm taking her to my house so she's protected, but I want to stop at her place first so she can get some belongings."

They all nod and disperse into two other SUVs as I round mine and climb in next to Cali. She's slumped against the seat, and I so badly want to unbuckle her and pull her onto my lap, but I also don't want to scare her. She's going through enough right now; she doesn't need me Daddying her out of the blue as well.

"Connor, we are going by Cali's to get some of her belongings before we go to my estate," I say.

Connor nods and starts driving, following the SUV that's leading us toward Cali's apartment. She doesn't seem to realize I already know where she lives, and I'm thankful for that at the moment.

When we pull up to her place, Connor parks, and she reaches for the door handle. I grab her wrist. "My men will let you out. Don't ever get out of the car unless they are there to see you out."

Her big brown eyes turn to me, and she looks as though she's going to argue or question me until Kieran opens her door and startles her.

"Sorry, lass. It's safe to get out," Kieran says, holding his hand out for her.

She moves to get out of the car, but her seatbelt is still on, and if this weren't such a serious situation, I'd chuckle at the pouty expression on her face as she glares at the latch. I reach over and push the button to release it. She looks up at me with appreciation.

"Thank you." Her voice is small and sad, and it makes the rage inside me burn even hotter. No one hurts my girl without feeling my wrath. I might not be able to keep her once all of this is done, but in my eyes, she's mine, and I'll burn the fucking world down just to make her happy.

I get out of the SUV and round it, going straight toward her. "We need to be in and out in ten minutes. I want you to grab anything and everything you need so you'll be comfortable at my home for a while."

She pulls her bottom lip between her teeth. "How long will I be there?"

"As long as needed, baby girl. Once we leave here today, we're not coming back until I know you're safe, so get everything you need. My men will help you."

Taking her by the elbow, I escort her into her apartment building with five of my men surrounding us. I know the inside of her building is secure because the security guard would call me immediately if anyone entered her apartment. But I don't know if the outside of her building is secure, so she has to come with me.

Maybe I'm taking this too far. Maybe I'm overreacting. But until I know more, I'm not taking any chances with her safety. The fact that she'll be in my home for a period of time where I can be close to her and get to know her is just an added bonus.

Once we're inside her apartment, I look around and can't help but smile. The whole place is extremely girly. There's pink stuff everywhere—blankets, a shit ton of throw pillows, twinkly lights strung up in the living room, a rug under the coffee table that looks like the fur from a polar bear, and candles on practically every surface. The corner of Killian's mouth twitches like he wants to smile too.

Ronan and Grady are walking around the apartment like they own the place, but I know they're doing a security sweep before we let her wander around on her own. When they come back to the living room and nod, I nudge her forward. "Go ahead and get what you need."

Cali heads for one of the bedrooms, and I immediately follow. I don't want her to be alone, and I want her near my side as much as possible. More pink. Lots of pink. And stuffed animals on her bed, which I find adorable. She looks up at me, and I see a hint of a blush on her cheeks. I want to reassure her that it's okay and tell her I'm a Daddy Dom so none of this cutesy stuff bothers me, but now isn't the time for that discussion.

"Do you have some bags?" I ask, trying to keep her on task.

She nods and digs two bags out of the closet, which are both, of course, pink.

"Give me one and fill the other with clothes."

I take one of the bags and go into the adjoining bathroom. Without asking, I start grabbing anything that seems to be a daily essential. Toothbrush, toothpaste, hairbrush, a small makeup bag, deodorant, body spray, and tampons. When I grab the tampons from the drawer, I notice something purple and long under them. A vibrator. My Little girl likes to pleasure herself. Fuck. The thought of that makes my cock thicken. Without a second thought, I reach into the drawer and grab the vibrator, only instead of sticking it in the bag, I put it in my suit pocket.

When I go back into her room, she's still grabbing clothes, so I go over to her bed. "Which stuffies do you want?"

She pauses and looks at me with uncertainty written all over her face.

"Pick some or I will," I tell her firmly.

"The wolf."

Every nerve in my body comes to life as I glance down and see a medium-sized stuffed wolf in front of all the other animals. How long has she had that? Did she get it after Halloween? The thought of her sleeping with that wolf every night and thinking about me makes my cock harden even more.

I ignore my cock, grab the wolf and two others—a bear and an elephant—and stuff them into the bag. When I look around her room again, I take inventory of all the stuff she has. I'll buy her whatever she needs to be comfortable, and it's obvious she's made her bedroom her safe space. There aren't any toys other than the stuffed animals, but everything else about her room screams Little. She might not be Little like some of the other women I know, but she's perfect for me.

"What else do you need, baby?"

Her shoulders droop as her bottom lip trembles. "I don't know. What am I even doing? I can't come stay with you. I don't even know you. This is crazy. You can't just move me into your house and let me interrupt your whole life."

In a flash, I'm in front of her, cupping her chin so she's forced to look up at me, and her watery eyes make my black heart crack right down the center. She feels uncertain and like a burden. I need to dominate her and take control so she doesn't feel guilty. "Baby girl, listen to me. You need to learn who the boss is here. Me. I decided you're coming to stay with me because I'm the boss and I say so. You'll be safe with me. I will never harm you. I want to help you. Understand?"

Her eyes search my face for several seconds before she nods. "Yes."

I don't let go of her chin. "Yes, Sir, would be better."

The air rushes out of her. Her chest starts to rise and fall faster. A sign that she likes what's happening here. She's not afraid of me like some people would be. No, the look on her face isn't fear. It's arousal. Thank fuck for that.

"Yes, Sir," she whispers.

"Good girl. Come on. Let's go home."

CALI'S quiet for the entire drive to my estate. I hate it. I want to see her beautiful smile and that mischievous look in her eyes I've seen before. Instead, she just looks defeated and completely exhausted. There are so many things I want to do to take care of her, but right now, I need to keep my distance and give her the help I promised.

When Connor pulls through the metal gates, her eyes widen. My house is set on ten acres just outside the city. The property is completely surrounded by stone walls and metal gates. I have security everywhere and armed guards at the entry gate. For me, it's normal. I'm sure for her it's terrifying, but she's safer here than at her apartment. My men will put their lives on the line to keep her safe because she's important to me.

"This is where you live?" she asks.

I nod. "Yes."

As we pull up to the round driveway with a large fountain in the center, she stares out the window toward my house. I can't tell if she likes it or hates it. When she reaches for the door handle, I grab her wrist again.

"Cali, do not open the car door," I say slowly and sternly. "My men make sure our surroundings are safe before they open them to let us out."

Her mouth drops open as she gapes at me. "But we're at your house."

"It doesn't matter. There's always risk. I mean it, Little girl."

She scrunches her face. "Risk of what? The seatbelt taking me out again?"

Connor chuckles as he tries to cover it with a cough, and I fight a smile myself at the little bit of fire she's showing. She's so damn cute.

Bash opens her door, and I meet his eyes. "Engage the child-proof lock. Apparently, this Little girl doesn't know how to wait."

Bash grins and clicks the locking mechanism into place. Cali gasps and looks at me with that fucking pout that makes me want to grab her by her hair and kiss those plump lips. It also makes me want to put her over my knee and spank her lush little bottom until she understands how serious I am about her safety.

"Seriously?" she asks.

I raise my eyebrows while Bash laughs, and I lean close to her ear so only she can hear me. "If you act like a naughty Little girl, I'm going to treat you like a naughty Little girl."

A shiver visibly runs through her body as she snaps her head back to meet my eyes, and I can see the mix of emotions running through her beautiful head. She loves what I said but she hates it too and wants to rebel. That's fine. She can rebel as much as she wants. I know how to deal with naughty girls like her, and I've been itching to feel her bottom under my palm for the past six months.

"Ready, lass? Or are you gonna sit in the car all day?" Bash asks.

I wink at her and get out on my side, ignoring Grady's smirk as I pass him. My guys are finding this humorous. Fuckers. They know how hung up I've been on her, and now with her here, I'm off my game. She stirs something inside me. It almost feels like I have a heart inside my chest. Almost.

7

CALI

Holy shit. I've never seen a house so big. This is bananas. I don't even know if "big" covers it. More like ginormous. It's stunning, though. Despite its size, it's beautifully built with stone and brick that gives it an old country feel. The windows have perfectly painted shutters, and the front porch, which is the size of a basketball court, has pots of flowers and rocking chairs perfectly set to make it feel inviting. It's definitely not the cold feel I would have expected from a mafia boss.

The landscape is so pretty. He must have at least a dozen gardeners working around the clock to keep the place this gorgeous. I can't help but notice all of the hydrangeas in various shades. They're my favorite.

My body is still buzzing over the words he whispered in my ear. I was so shocked, I couldn't speak. My pussy responded, though. I'm pretty sure my panties are done for. Might as well just throw them away at this point.

Declan is so stern sometimes and so kind and sweet other times. I know he's a criminal and runs an entire illegal organization. I'm under no delusion he's not dangerous. I've read enough mafia books and seen enough mafia movies to know this man has blood on his hands. Lots and lots of blood most likely. I should be afraid of him. I should be afraid of all of them. They're tall and muscular, and when they have their stern expressions in place, they look freaking terrifying. For some reason, I'm not scared.

Bash is still smirking at me as he helps me out of the car. I like him. I like Killian too. I haven't really interacted with the others. I don't even know their names. Am I crazy? I'm willingly walking into a mobster's house. Maybe I am, but I'll do anything to find my sister. Even though these guys are gangsters, I have a feeling deep in my gut that they aren't going to hurt me.

I wonder where my sister is right now. What is she doing? Is she hurt? Is she even alive? I hate that these questions are going through my mind, but it's the reality of the situation.

Declan stays beside me as we enter the house, and I'm immediately in awe of the interior. The foyer is enormous with a grand staircase that leads to the second floor. There are several hallways leading in different directions. I'm surprised at how tastefully decorated it is. Despite being so large, it feels warm and comfortable inside. Like a home should. I would have used more pink, but I suspect that isn't Declan's color.

"I'll show you to your room so you can get settled, and then we need to meet with my men and get some more information about your sister," Declan says.

His warm hand presses against my lower back, and he leads me up the staircase. With each step, I feel my exhaustion all the way down to my bones. I sway a little, and Declan wraps his arm around my waist to steady me.

"Grab hold of the railing, baby."

I obey and hold the railing as we make our way upstairs with his arm still wrapped around me. He's warm and soothing, and I want to curl into him and hide in his embrace forever, but I don't expect he'd appreciate that. He's being kind and calling me sweet names, but I'm pretty sure he feels sorry for me. I feel sorry for dropping my problems in his lap, but he's the only resource I have.

He opens a set of French doors that lead into a bedroom the size of my entire apartment. One of his men follows us and silently leaves my bags near the door before he disappears.

I've never seen a room like this. There's a king-size bed, plus a whole living room set, and there's still a bunch of open space. The rug is so plush, I'm afraid to walk on it with my shoes on, but he doesn't seem to have the same hesitation as he ushers me in.

"My bedroom is the next door down."

I nod, though I'm not sure why he told me that. "Thank you. This is...too much."

"Nothing is ever too much for you. Get settled. Have you eaten today?"

The question makes me lower my gaze. I'm pretty sure my answer won't please him. "No."

"When was the last time you ate, Cali?"

I shrug. "I'm not sure. The past few days have been a blur."

He steps closer to me and cups my chin. My eyes meet his, and though I can tell he isn't thrilled with my answer, he doesn't look angry. He stares at me, and for a moment, I think he's going to kiss me, but then he drops his hand and steps back. "When you're settled, come downstairs and someone will show you where my office is. If you need anything, there's an intercom by the door. The red button will connect you to my office, and the green button will connect you to one of the staff who can get you whatever you need."

Before I can say anything, he walks out of the room and gently closes the door behind him.

I STILL CAN'T GET over this room. The walk-in closet is bigger than my bedroom. It's beautiful, though. I can't imagine living in such an extraordinary house. I might only be here for a few days, but I'm going to enjoy it as much as I can.

After I change out of my work dress and put on a pair of soft leggings and an oversized sweatshirt that has seen better days, I sit on the bed and look at my phone. A picture of Scarlet and me down at the waterfront is on my lock screen, and I can't stop the sob that escapes. My sister. She's been the only constant in my life, and now we're both alone to fend for ourselves. We need each other. Some people go to therapy. We go to each other. That's our therapy.

A knock at the door startles me, but I put my phone down and answer it. The man on the other side always comes to the pub with Declan, but I don't know his name. He's handsome, though I'm not drawn to him like I am to Declan. They have similar features, and I wonder if they're related.

"I came to see if you're ready to come downstairs," he says.

I nod and lower my gaze. It's now or never, I guess. To say I'm nervous about going into a room full of gangsters is an understatement.

He chuckles, making me look up at him again.

"Don't worry, lass. We don't bite. Not usually."

His humor soothes me. I'm still slightly terrified of him, though. The man looks like he tears people apart for fun. I do like that these men who look so serious all the time have a lighter side to them that they only seem to show to each other and apparently, me. I still need to be cautious. I don't want to become fishy bait.

"Okay. I'm ready."

"I'm Ronan, by the way. Declan and Bash are my brothers. Not sure if you knew that," he says before turning and walking down the hall. I follow him.

Somehow, knowing his name makes me feel better. "Nice to meet you. Sorry...for all of this."

My gaze darts all around the hall, taking in the neutral colors and tasteful art until I crash into Ronan's back. I didn't see him stop mid-stride. Before I fall on my ass, he has a hold of my arms, keeping me on my feet. His eyebrows furrow, and I see the disapproval in his eyes. "Don't apologize. This isn't your fault. Whoever took your sister, it's on them. We're all glad you came to us. My brother especially."

Why would Declan be especially glad I went to him? I don't have time to think about it because Ronan shifts his grip and leads me downstairs, then through a wide hall. When he turns, I freeze. There are at least a dozen terrifying-looking men in black suits sitting around a large table.

Declan rises from his seat, coming toward me. He leans down close to my ear. "It's okay, Little one. No one in here is going to hurt you. I'd never allow it."

The way he whispers to me feels so intimate. Words only meant for me. I look into his eyes and melt a little. How can one man be so stunningly gorgeous? I have no idea if he's even single. I can't imagine someone like him would be. Then again, he probably has a whole herd of women lining up to date him. I wonder if I can get in line too, but the thought makes me roll my eyes. Like he would ever want me.

"Did you just roll your eyes at me?" he asks with a raised brow.

Shit.

"Sorry, no. I...I had something in my eye, I think. It's better now."

He knows I'm lying, but he doesn't call me out on it. Instead, he puts his hand on my lower back, leads me to the head of the table, and pulls out the chair. I wait for him to take a seat, but he motions toward me. "Sit."

My eyes widen. He wants me to sit at the head of the table? I'm nobody. Just a girl. Isn't that his spot?

"Cali, sit. Now." His words are firm but quiet enough I don't think the other men hear the command.

I sit, and he pushes me in so I'm right up at the table with him standing next to me.

"This is Cali Jenkins," he says to the room before looking down at me. "I've already briefed them on the situation, but now we need you to give us more information."

Declan wraps his hand around the back of my neck, and it feels possessive in a way, but I think he's doing it to reassure me. Whatever it is, I like it, and I don't want him to stop.

"Cali, I'm Grady," a man with cold, green eyes says. "You told Declan someone from the mafia took your sister. Do you have any idea who he is?"

I peer up at Declan, who gives me a single nod. I'm not sure why I'm looking to him for permission, but I feel like I need it. "I'm pretty sure he's in the Russian mob. My sister had been dating him for the past eight months or so. She dumped him because he's been treating her badly. He told her she'd regret breaking up with someone like him, but we thought he meant because he was rich or something."

All of the men's faces harden, and the tension in the air feels so thick, it's hard to breathe. It's obvious the Russian mafia is a sore point for these men.

"Do you know his name?" Killian asks.

I twist my fingers together in my lap. "I only know his first name. It's Ivan."

Declan's fingers tighten around the back of my neck, and I know without even looking at him that he's pissed.

8

DECLAN

Cali shifts under my hand, and I realize I'm squeezing the sides of her neck. I relax my grip and look at my men. They're as close to exploding as I am.

"Ivan Petrov? Young, in his twenties, blond hair?" I ask.

She looks up at me with wide, frightened eyes and nods. "Yes."

I stare down at her for a long moment and notice her bottom lip tremble, which just pisses me off more. I already hated the guy, but now, I want to fucking kill him. He's causing my girl pain, and he's just some kid with an ego. What her sister ever saw in the guy, I don't know.

"As of now, Cali is on lockdown. She goes nowhere without guards. Not even out to the pool by herself. Cullen, start digging. I'll call a meeting with Vladimir. He's still the one in power, so hopefully, he will make the right choice."

"Aye, boss," Cullen replies as he gets up from his seat and disappears from the room.

"Everyone out," I snap.

Cali jumps at my sharp words and then starts to rise from the chair, but I put my hand on her shoulder. "Not you."

Her eyes widen but she stays put.

"Killian, you stay, too," I say.

Killian nods and stays seated in the chair to the right of Cali. Once we're the only three left, I take a seat next to her. I know she's uneasy about sitting at the head of the table, but she doesn't say anything as she looks back and forth at us with an uneasy expression.

I sigh heavily and run my hand over my chin as I study her. She's trembling, and I know she's exhausted. I also need to get her to eat something. But first, I need to be honest with her.

"Cali," I say softly.

She raises her gaze to mine, and it's the saddest thing I've ever seen.

"I'm going to do everything in my power to save your sister. I'm going to be honest with you, though. I don't know what the outcome will be, considering who took her."

Tears well in her eyes, so I reach out and pull her hand to mine. "No matter what, I promise to avenge you and your sister."

"Do you think he's killed her?" she asks so quietly I can barely hear.

I look at Killian. He's thinking the same thing I am. It's entirely possible Scarlet is already dead, but I can't bring myself to tell my Little girl that.

"I don't know. I hope not. As soon as I know anything, I will tell you. I need you to try to keep a positive mind. Scarlet needs as many good thoughts as possible at this point. Can you be strong for her?"

Even though tears are falling down her cheeks and her shoulders are slumped, she nods. "Yes. Of course. Always."

Her answer makes me think she's had to be strong for way too long, for both herself and her sister. That's going to change. She's going to learn what it's like for someone else to take care of her for once.

"Here's an untraceable cell phone. My number is programmed in there, along with Killian, Bash, Ronan, Grady, and Kieran. If you need anything at all and I'm not available, you can trust any of these men. Understand?" I slide the brand new phone over to her.

She eyes it and then raises her gaze to me. "Why are you doing all of this? Helping me?"

I study her face for a long moment, trying to decide how much I want to tell her. "Because I like you, Cali. I've liked you since the moment I laid eyes on you, and I care about keeping you safe. I have no tolerance for hurting women."

Although I didn't tell her much, I did speak the truth. She just doesn't know the first time I laid eyes on her was six months ago at Surrender and not at O'Leary's.

She wipes her tears with the back of her hands and smiles. "Thank you. This means so much to me. I've been so scared and feeling so helpless. She's my best friend, and she's the only person in my life who has ever really meant something to me."

That makes my chest ache. Why didn't she have parents who meant something to her? Why was this Little girl forced to be so strong?

"We'll find her," Killian says firmly.

Cali looks at him and gives him a sad smile. "Thank you. I don't know how I'll ever pay you guys back."

Killian grins at her. "It's so cute that you think we'd let you pay us back, lass. Cute as a little mouse."

His words make her narrow her eyes at him, and I chuckle. She might be emotional, but there's still fire in her, and I love it.

"Mice have big ugly red eyes, so what are you trying to say? If I'm a mouse, what does that make you? A big...a big...butthead! Yeah, are you a big butthead?"

Killian chuckles and shakes his head, letting her comment roll right off his back. He likes her fire too.

I barely keep myself from laughing as I speak up. "There will be no paying us back or name calling, Cali. Just obey my rules, and let my men keep you safe. Understand?"

She turns her attention to me, and I can see her pupils dilate. Whether she realizes it or not, she likes the idea of obeying me. Or maybe she likes the thought of disobeying me. I'm fine with either. If she's a good girl, I'll praise her and spoil her, and if she's naughty, I'll turn her bottom red. Both scenarios make my cock thicken.

"I understand," she replies quietly.

"Good girl."

The corners of her mouth pull back into a soft, genuine smile, and it makes me want to keep praising her if it means I get to keep seeing her like this.

I look at Killian. "Arrange a meeting with Vladimir outside of both our territories."

Killian nods. "Aye."

As I rise from my chair, I reach out and take Cali's hand. "And you, Little girl, are coming with me to the kitchen to find something to eat."

She follows me out of the room, and I'm pleased when she doesn't try to pull her hand away. The need to touch her is so damn strong, and it keeps getting worse by the second. Once all of this is over and she goes back to her regular life, I'll be a shell of a man, but it's worth the time I get to spend with her.

My head housekeeper, Grace, is in the kitchen when we enter. She's already been briefed about Cali, so she isn't surprised it's not just me coming in.

"Grace, this is Cali. Cali, this is Grace. She's the head housekeeper, and if you need anything, she'll be able to get it for you."

Grace smiles warmly at Cali. "It's nice to meet you. Are you hungry? I made some stew earlier and it's still hot."

Cali looks up at me, and I love that she defers to me. It's a turn on like no other. I nod at Grace. "Yes, please. Only for Cali. I'm not hungry."

I lead Cali out of the kitchen to an informal dining area and pull out a chair for her at the small bistro table. She looks so tiny, and when I sit down next to her, I fight the urge to pull her onto my lap.

Grace brings out a bowl of stew and some bread, along with a glass of water. "I'll be in the kitchen if you need anything else."

As soon as she disappears from the room, I turn my attention to Cali who's looking at the bowl of soup with uncertainty.

"You need to eat, baby."

Her eyes rise to meet mine. "I don't know if I can."

I study her for a few seconds before I scoot my chair closer to her and pick up the bowl of stew. Scooping up a small spoonful, I bring it up to my lips to test the temperature before I move it to her mouth. "Open. You have to eat a little bit at least."

She keeps her eyes locked on mine as she opens her mouth so I can feed her. It's erotic, and all I can think about is her opening those lips for my cock. When she lets out a small moan of appreciation for the stew, I nearly groan. Fuck. I want to hear those sweet little sounds as I feast on her pussy or fuck her mouth.

Forcing myself to ignore my own perverse thoughts, I scoop up another spoonful, making sure to get a piece of meat so she gets a little protein. She automatically opens her lips as I lift the spoon to them.

"Good girl," I murmur.

"Don't you have more important things to be doing than feeding me?"

I look her dead in the eye. "No. I don't."

Her eyes widen, clearly surprised by my answer, but it's the truth. Nothing is more important than taking care of her.

She lowers her gaze, and I see a hint of a smile as she stares into the bowl. "Never thought a mob boss would be spoon-feeding me."

I smile. "Sometimes people are different than what you expect."

"I guess so."

My phone buzzes in my pocket, and when I see the message from Killian, I clench my jaw. Vladimir agreed to a meeting tonight.

"Come on, I want you to eat some more, and then I want you to go to bed. I'm going to be gone tonight, but Bash and Grady will be here."

She watches me as I lift the spoon to her mouth again. A line of broth drips down her chin, so I grab her napkin and wipe it off before she has the chance. Her mouth falls open as my thumb brushes over her bottom lip. It kills me to pull away from her, but I need to keep my control in check. She's exhausted, emotionally drained, and upset. She needs my care right now, not my dick.

"Where are you going tonight?"

I wonder why she's asking. Is it just curiosity, or is it something more? Jealousy? I doubt it, but I wouldn't hate it if she were jealous.

"Killian and I are flying to Colorado to meet with Vladimir Petrov. He's the head of the Russian Mafia. I'll be home by morning. You can reach me by phone anytime, though."

Her eyes widen again. "You're flying to Colorado to meet with him?"

"Yes. He lives in Chicago. We're meeting in neutral territory."

I continue to feed her as we talk, and I'm glad she's eating. It might not be much, but it's something. She'll be eating on a regular basis while she's in my home.

"How did you get a flight so fast?"

Her question makes me chuckle. She has no idea how fortunate I am. "I own a private jet. I can fly anywhere at a moment's notice."

She stares at the table, and I can tell she's trying to work something out in her mind. When she finally speaks, her voice is strained. "Can I go too? Maybe if I could talk to him, he'd let her go?"

"Look at me." I wait until she raises her gaze to meet mine. "It's not safe for you. What I need you to do is go to bed and sleep. You need to rest, baby girl. Can you please do that for me?"

I'm asking even though it's not a question. She will go to bed, and she will rest, even if I have to have one of my men sit in her room and make sure she stays tucked in.

"I'll try. I don't know if I can sleep."

When I hold another spoonful of stew up to her mouth, she scrunches her nose and shakes her head. "I can't eat anymore."

"Okay. Come on." I rise and hold out my hand for her, waiting until she takes it and follows me through the house.

Once we're upstairs, I lead her into her room and walk over to the bed, pulling the bedding down. "Go get changed into some pajamas. I'll wait here."

She stares at me, frozen in place like she isn't sure what to do.

"Do you need my help getting changed?" I ask.

Her eyes widen, and she quickly shakes her head before she scurries off into the bathroom and closes the door behind her.

I sit on the bed and wait for her to return to me, where she belongs. I may not be helping her get her pajamas on, or doing any of the other things she needs to do to get ready for bed, but at least I get to tuck her in. She needs sleep, and I'm hoping with some food in her tummy and my reassurance that I'm going to do everything I can to find her sister that she'll be able to finally rest.

When the bathroom door opens, I can't breathe. She's wearing a matching pajama set that's pink, of course, but it has tiny hearts printed all over the shorts and tank top. Her hair is loose, and her face is scrubbed free of makeup. Even though she always looks young, she looks even younger now and so fucking innocent. Guilt fills me for the filthy thoughts I have about her. She's too sweet and pure, and I'm too corrupt and dangerous. I have no business wanting her, but I can't stop.

"Come here." My voice is gravelly so I clear my throat. My body feels like it's on fire, and she's not even naked.

Cali shuffles toward the bed and climbs under the covers, pulling them up over her smooth legs that I want to run my tongue over. She's sitting up, and she looks nervous. I want to soothe all of her fears, but since I don't know what the severity of the situation is yet, I won't make false promises.

"I want you to sleep, Little one. You're exhausted, and right now, there's nothing you can do to help, so staying up and worrying won't do you any good. Understand?"

Her wide brown eyes meet mine. "I'm not usually this helpless. I just didn't know what else to do. I'm used to taking care of everything myself."

That simple statement makes my heart ache. She's been taking care of herself and Scarlet for way too long. It's time for that to stop.

"You're not helpless, Cali. Since the first time I saw you, I knew you were strong. Just because you came to me doesn't make you any less."

"You noticed me when you first saw me?" Her face scrunches up as soon as the words are out as though she regrets saying them, but I'm glad she asked.

"Since the first time I laid eyes on you, I knew you were special. I haven't stopped looking at you since, Little one."

A soft smile spreads across her face, and I think she likes what I've told her. Even though we have no future, I want her to know how amazing she is.

"Are you always this nice?"

I can't help but smile at the question, but I look her directly in the eye. "No. In fact, I'm never this nice. I guess you bring it out in me."

Her chest rises and falls a little faster. She wasn't expecting that answer. Interesting. I reach over, grab the stuffed wolf from the foot of the bed, and hand it to her. "What's his name?"

A blush rises to her cheeks, and she lowers her gaze from mine but smiles as she looks down at the stuffed animal. "His name is Snickers."

And just like that, the air is knocked from my lungs. I'm a goner for this Little girl. I don't know if I'll have the strength to let her go after all of this is over.

I can't stop myself from reaching out to brush her hair away from her face. "It's time to sleep. I'll be here when you wake up in the morning."

She nods and lowers herself onto the pillows, and I immediately notice her pointed nipples under the thin fabric of her tank top. My mouth dries up like the desert. It's torture, but I force my gaze away from her chest to meet her eyes. "Sweet dreams, Little one."

As I pull the blankets up over her, she smiles softly and tucks the stuffed wolf under her arm. "Night, Declan. Be careful, okay?"

Her voice is so damn small and innocent, and her words make me wonder if she would actually care if something happened to me. For the first time in my life, I want someone to care. It's not a feeling I'm used to. In this life, there's always the possibility of death, and it's something I made peace with when I was just a boy. But now, I'm not so sure I'm ready to leave this world. Not without her.

9

CALI

I can't sleep. I can't stop thinking, and I feel a little guilty because I should only be thinking about my sister. She hasn't left my mind since she went missing. But I'm also thinking about the gorgeous green-eyed gangster who makes my heart pound in my chest and my pussy ache with a need I've never felt before.

When I can't take it anymore, I throw the covers back and sit up in bed. Declan told me to make myself at home, and when he took me to the kitchen earlier, I noticed a cozy-looking living room. The house is so big I'm not sure I'll find it again, but I need something to do other than what I've been doing for the past two hours. I can only stare at the ceiling for so long.

I feel silly, but I grab Snickers to take with me. Even though he's just my stuffed toy, he makes me feel safer. It's ridiculous, but I know who I am and what I am, and Declan doesn't seem to mind that I have a toy. Lots of people sleep with stuffies. Right?

The house is quiet as I make my way downstairs. I notice two men standing at the front door, but they don't say anything to me. Instead they nod while keeping their terrifying expressions in place. I'm pretty sure someone would have to have a death wish to break into this house. These two men look like they could snap necks with their bare hands. I scurry out of the foyer as quickly as possible to get away from them.

It takes me a few minutes, but I find the living room, and when I walk in, I pause. Bash and Grady sit on opposite couches with the TV on, though neither of them seems to be watching it. They're in the middle of a conversation, but when they notice me, they stop talking and look at me.

"You okay, lass?" Grady asks, standing with his eyebrows furrowed.

I nod and offer him a smile, which seems to pacify him because he slowly sits back down. The man is enormous, and I almost giggle because even though he's sitting on a full-size couch, he practically takes up half of it.

"You're supposed to be in bed sleeping, Little one," Bash says.

I ignore him as I walk into the room and sit across from Grady, then tuck Snickers down by my thigh, hoping not to draw attention to him. Bash smirks at me. He's probably not used to people ignoring him, but I'm still annoyed over the child-lock thing. Big buffoon.

"What are you guys watching?" I ask. It's a silly question because I can clearly see they have the news on.

Grady grabs the remote control and tosses it to me. "Turn it to whatever you want, lass. We're not really watching anything."

I give Bash a sassy smirk in return before I start channel surfing. Neither of them talk, and I feel bad that I interrupted their conversation, but I also feel better being around them. I continue flipping through channels, and when I find *Beauty and the Beast*, I stop and put the remote down, then glance at the two terrifying men to see if they're judging me, but there's nothing but approval in their gazes.

"Couldn't sleep?" Grady finally asks.

"No. I tried. I can't stop thinking about Scarlet. I miss her, and I'm worried about her. Have you heard anything from Declan?"

Bash rises, and I'm surprised when he grabs a throw blanket from the back of the couch and settles it over my body. Okay, maybe he's not so bad. One brownie point for him. Though, he got two taken away for his stunt earlier so he's still sitting in the negative.

"Want some cocoa?" he asks.

Damn. Another point for him.

I shake my head. "No, thank you."

Bash rests his elbows on his knees. "Declan is still in the air. He won't touch down in Denver for another hour. He won't be happy you're not sleeping."

The warmth from the blanket soothes me, and I feel myself sinking into the plush couch, my eyes heavy as I try to watch the movie. Something about being around these guys is making me feel safe, and my mind is quiet for the first time in hours. I give Bash a sleepy smile. "Is he going to cut off one of my fingers if I displease him?" I murmur. "Hopefully he chooses a finger I don't like or maybe a toe. Yeah, I don't like my pinky toe. He can cut off that one."

Both Bash and Grady laugh and shake their heads, but the sleep I've been missing is finally catching up to me, and I slowly drift off, the sound of the movie and the men's voices drowning out all other thoughts.

10

DECLAN

The minute Killian and I walk into the strip club—along with half a dozen of my men—I want to leave. The dancers see us and can tell we have endless amounts of cash, and suddenly, we're being stalked through the club as we make our way back to the VIP room we have reserved. We have to pry hands away as endless half-naked women offer us private dances. Their touches make my skin crawl. They're beautiful women, but they aren't Cali.

I don't want to be here. I want to be at home with the sweet Little girl who has crept her way into my heart. She needs her sister, though, and I want to give Cali everything she could ever want or need. Which is why I'm at this shitty strip club meeting Vladimir.

When I walk into the room, I tense. I'd asked to meet with Vladimir and his underboss alone, but Ivan is sitting next to his father with a smug look on his face. I don't like this guy.

Vladimir rises from his chair and holds out his meaty hand. "Declan. Nice to see you again. Killian."

We both shake his hand. When Ivan doesn't rise to offer the same niceties, I sit and focus my attention on Vlad who is looking at his son with a disapproving expression.

"You know my son, Ivan. Nikoli couldn't make it tonight. His wife is in labor," Vladimir offers.

I nod. That explains why his underboss isn't here, but I still don't like that Ivan is here in his place. Especially since I know this little fucker is the one who took Cali's sister. I want to grab him by the throat and break his neck with my bare hands.

"Thank you for meeting with me on such short notice. I've been made aware of a situation that may need the attention of our organizations," I say, trying avoid any kind of direct accusation.

I sit across from the two men, though what I really want to do is turn this fucking table over and put a bullet between Ivan's eyes. Unfortunately, that would start an immediate war, and that's exactly what I'm trying to avoid.

Vladimir's eyebrows furrow while Ivan looks at us with complete disinterest. His lack of respect makes me grind my molars together. I already know this kid is going to destroy his father's legacy and ruin everything we've worked so hard to build. Relationships will be severed and business agreements will be broken. Making this kid the Russian mob boss is a ticking time bomb.

"What kind of situation?" Vladimir asks.

I level my gaze at the older man. "A woman was kidnapped, and we're trying to find her. We believe she was taken by one of the syndicates."

This makes Ivan sit up a little straighter, a move he doesn't realize confirms his guilt. Killian sees it too. I'm smiling on the inside over the fact that this fucker just gave himself away.

Vlad's eyebrows shoot up, which tells me he's not aware

of what his son has done. That makes me feel a little better. Ivan might not give a fuck about the pact between the families, but Vlad is still holding true to it.

"We don't hurt women. It's been a pact held for over thirty years. Who has broken the agreement?" Vladimir asks.

"We're not sure yet. That's what we're trying to find out," I reply before adding, "She belongs to us."

That statement causes Ivan's face to pale slightly, but he quickly regains his composure, probably hoping I didn't see his reaction. Ivan might not be ruling the Russian Mafia yet, but he knows breaking the pact would be damaging, but breaking the pact *and* taking a woman who belongs to another family would mean war.

"I'm sure you understand this is something we don't take lightly. At this point, we're hoping this is just a misunderstanding and she'll be returned to us unscathed. No harm, no foul," I say.

Vladimir nods, looking thoughtful before he meets my gaze again. "Are you insinuating she was taken by us?"

I lean back in my seat, and even though I can feel the thick tension in the air, I shrug my shoulders nonchalantly. "I'm just asking around at this point, but I have reason to believe she might have been involved with someone from your organization."

The older man turns to Ivan and starts speaking in Russian. Ivan shakes his head and is obviously brushing his father's questions off. When they finish their conversation, Vladimir turns back to me. "I assure you if this is happening inside my organization, I am not aware of it and I would not approve of such a thing."

For the first time, I notice the fatigue under Vladimir's eyes and the extra worry lines around his face. I suspect he knows his son is disrespecting the organization he's worked so hard to build. If I were a better man, I might feel sorry for him. I'm not, though. I'm a monster, and while I might maintain the pact and relationships we've built, I'm always going to look out for myself and my men first.

"While I respect that, you do understand anything that happens within your organization involving the disappearance of someone in my family—whether or not you're aware of it—is not something I can ignore."

I can feel the tension growing around us, and Ivan stands so suddenly that his father looks up at him. Killian rises, ready to fight at the drop of a hat. This is one of the many reasons why he's my second in command. Killian's loyalty has never wavered, and he'd put his life before mine if it came down to it. I'm not sure if he realizes it, but I'd do the same for him.

"Are you threatening us? I don't think that would bode very well for you and your men," Ivan snaps.

Since I know Killian will be keeping his eyes on Ivan, I move my gaze back to his father. "Respectfully, Vladimir, you know what breaking the pact means for the family who breaks it, especially in this way. You worked with my father for a long time, and you know I'm just like him. I don't make idle threats. I respect you and the relationship we've built over the years. It's a relationship I'd like to continue."

Vlad nods. "I agree. If I have someone in my ranks who is going against the pact or hurting a woman, they will be dealt with swiftly. This is the first I've heard of this matter, so I need a few days to look inside my organization."

I rise and look at Ivan. "Her name is Scarlet Jenkins. I'm giving you twenty-four hours, and if she's not released within that time, I'll be forced to take further action."

Ivan's eyes narrow the second I say her name, and I know without a doubt he's the one responsible for taking Scarlet.

Vladimir rises and looks a bit rattled. He understands the

consequences if he doesn't figure out who took her. He knows the bloodshed that will follow if we start a war. He's been through a mafia war before. He doesn't want it to happen again. None of us do. Which is why the pact is in place. Unfortunately, his weasel of a son doesn't hold the same respect for it.

"You're sure she's been taken by someone in my ranks?" Vladimir asks.

"Yes, Vlad. I'm sure. And with all due respect," I say as I move my gaze to Ivan and then back to Vladimir, "you might want to look at the people closest to you first."

Understanding fills the older man's eyes, and for just a moment, I try to understand how he must feel to learn his only son is destroying what he worked so hard to build. To have his own son break the very pact he signed off on so many years ago and to disgrace his legacy must be heart-breaking. I almost feel bad for the older man.

I turn and walk out of the room, Killian following me, and I can hear Ivan rapidly speaking to his father in Russian. I don't want to start a war. It's the last thing any sane mafia boss would want. But when it comes to Cali, I have no sanity, and I'll do whatever it takes to get her sister back so my girl can be happy again.

I'm SEETHING the entire flight home. Killian seems to be in the same mood. We both wanted to kill Ivan on sight, but we need to be cautious and not start a war right out of the gate. If Scarlet is returned to Cali unharmed and Ivan—along with any of his goons who helped kidnap her—are handled by Vladimir, I'm willing to keep the pact for the sake of all the syndicate families. I understand what a war would do to everyone involved. My father always told me it should only come as a last resort, but once it starts, you don't back down until you win or die. I'll follow that advice for the rest of my life.

"He fucking has her. I could see it. She's alive. I don't know how I know, I just know," Killian finally says.

We've been sitting across from each other in silence while sipping whiskey and gathering our thoughts. My other men are spread throughout the plane, talking amongst themselves.

"What makes you say that?"

He shrugs. "There was something in his eye. Even though he was acting pissed, I could see his wheels turning. Like he was weighing what you said about setting her free. Call it a feeling, but she's alive. We just have to find her."

I nod and take a sip of my drink. I trust Killian's gut. He has the best instincts of anyone I've ever met. "Spread the word to tighten up security. Now that they know we're looking into them, we need to be prepared for retaliation."

Killian nods and starts tapping away on his phone while I count down the minutes until I can get home and see my girl. What would she think knowing I consider her mine? Would she like it? Or would she be scared? Pissed? Annoyed? Do I want to know the answer? I'm not sure how I'd handle it if she rejects me.

It's nearly five in the morning by the time we get home. I go directly to the living room. Bash texted me a few hours ago to tell me she'd come down and had fallen asleep on the couch. He asked if I wanted him to move her up to her room, but I told him to leave her. That's my job, and the thought of anyone other than me tucking her in makes me murderous.

When I walk into the living room, my eyes immediately go to her. Bash and Grady are watching the morning news on mute with subtitles, and Cali is curled up in a tight ball with her stuffed wolf clutched to her chest and a blanket wrapped around her. She looks so precious and peaceful.

Occasionally her nose scrunches up or her lips twitch like she's having a dream. I hope it's a pleasant one.

As soon as the guys notice me, they turn off the TV and disappear from the room, leaving me alone with Cali. I sit beside her and gently brush some hair away from her face.

She stirs. "Declan," she whispers without even opening her eyes.

"Aye, baby. It's me. Why aren't you in bed like I told you to be?"

She scrunches her cute little nose. "You didn't tell me to stay in bed. You told me to sleep. I'm sleeping."

I grin, and I'm glad her eyes aren't open because though she's amusing me, I don't want her to think she can find workarounds for my rules or instructions. "You're naughty. What am I going to do with you?"

A soft smile spreads on her lips. "You told me you'd never harm me, so I know you won't cut off my fingers."

I blink several times as her words settle and then chuckle because, what the fuck? "Baby, do you think I go around cutting people's fingers off for fun?"

"I've read mafia books," she murmurs.

All I can do is shake my head. I stand and slide one arm under her knees and one under her lower back, lifting her and heading toward her bedroom. "I think you've been reading some weird mafia books. I've never cut off a finger in my life."

Her brows furrow, but her eyes are still closed, and she's snuggling into my chest. "That sounds boring. Have you pulled people's teeth out with pliers?"

Now I'm laughing because I don't know if she's so tired she has no idea what she's saying or if she's really asking.

"No teeth and no pliers, baby. I don't think I want you reading mafia books anymore. They really make us look bad."

She lets out a deep sigh. "You're too handsome to look bad. Why do you smell so good?"

My cock surges to life in my slacks as I carry her into her bedroom. She's killing me. When I set her down on the bed, she sighs again, and within seconds, her breathing evens out. She probably won't remember the words that just came out of her mouth, but I will. I'll never forget them.

11

CALI

Before I even open my eyes, I know he's in the room. I can smell his cologne. It's fresh and citrusy but has intense undertones that make him smell so edible, I can hardly stand it. I wonder if he tastes as good as he smells. I'm sure he does. He probably looks like a Greek god when he's naked, too. Based on all the tattoos on his hands and forearms, I'm pretty sure his chest and biceps are covered in ink too. I'd like to trace those lines with my tongue. The thought causes me to let out a soft moan, and then I remember he's in the room with me.

My eyes fly open to find him sitting in a chair near the bed, his elbows resting on his knees. He's smirking at me. I should be embarrassed by the noise I made, but all I can focus on is the fact that his suit jacket is thrown over the back of the chair and his black button-down shirt has the sleeves rolled up to his elbows and the first several buttons undone, leaving me a slight glimpse of the chest I was just thinking about licking.

"Good dream, baby?"

God. His voice is smooth like honey but deep and thick. The things he could make me do with just that voice would be embarrassing to admit. But not only is it sexy, it makes me feel safe in a way I've never felt before. I don't really know what to think about that. I shouldn't like someone like him. He's dangerous, cocky, a criminal, and he could have any woman he wants. Those things should all turn me off, but instead, they do the opposite.

Moments pass and I don't answer him, but our eyes lock and we're having this intimate moment. I wish I could ask him to get into bed and hold me. I need some strong arms to comfort me.

When I remember where he went last night, I sit up and brush my wild nest of hair away from my face. Hopefully, I don't have drool on my chin.

"Did you find Scarlet?"

I can tell by the look in his eyes the answer is no, and my heart sinks.

"No. But we're pretty sure she's still alive."

His words hit me like a bullet. They could still kill her, and I'd never see my sister again. I try to remember the last words I said to her. Did I tell her I loved her? I can't remember, and that makes me cry.

Declan moves to the edge of my bed in a flash and pulls me onto his lap, his thick arms wrapping around me.

"I've got you, baby. Shh. We're working on it. I have a feeling the meeting we had last night will result in something good. I promise I won't give up until we find her."

I nod against his chest but don't speak because the lump in my throat is too big and painful for me to even try. I just let him hold me. It's soothing and even though he probably has a million other things he needs to be doing, he's sitting here holding me. That means more to me than I could ever explain.

My fingers find the edge of his shirt, and I grab hold of it. The back of my hand rests on his chest, and he stops breathing for a few seconds. It makes me wonder if he feels the same electricity between us that I do. I hope so.

"What do we do now?" I finally ask.

He continues to stroke my back, his chin resting on the top of my head. "I'll continue to search, and you're going to relax, watch movies, eat whatever you wish, and come to me anytime you need to be held."

His words make me smile. "I can't just come to you when I want to be held. You have to work."

Declan pulls back so he's looking me directly in the eye. "You come to me anytime. I don't care if I'm asleep, in a meeting, working out, eating, or anything else, you come to me. I'll be upset if you don't. Understood?"

His expression is so stern, I can't do anything but nod, and that seems to satisfy him because he smiles and pulls me back against his chest.

"You might get tired of how often I need comfort," I murmur after a few minutes.

"Not a chance, Little girl. I'll hold you all day if you let me."

Let him? Of course I'd let him. But that would be weird, right? A shiver runs through me, and my mind wanders to all his sweet nicknames for me. Particularly Little girl.

"Why do you always call me Little girl?" I blurt.

His hand stills on my back and then starts moving a few seconds later. "You're Little, aren't you?"

My eyes widen, and I pull back to look up at him. How does he know? Am I that obvious?

He chuckles, then stands with me in his arms like I weigh nothing and starts walking out of the room.

"Where are we going?"

"I'm going to show you something."

Should I be excited or worried? I have no idea. I hope he's going to show me his cock, but I have a feeling that isn't it. Disappointing.

When he walks into the room he told me was his, I look around and take in a deep breath. It smells like him. The décor is masculine and tasteful. I thought the room I was staying in was big. This one is about twice that size. Everything matches, and the earthy colors of the room make it feel soothing.

He walks over to the massive bed and sets me down on the edge, then puts his hands on either side of my hips, caging me in. His face is only inches from mine as he leans down, and I wonder if he's going to kiss me. I want him to. So badly it hurts. My core aches and my panties are damp.

"I told you that you captured my attention the first time I saw you," he says before he straightens and reaches for the bedside table.

My eyes follow his movements as he opens the drawer and pulls out something small, wrapping it in his hand so I can't see what it is. When he comes back, he stares down at me with so much intensity, I shiver until he opens his hand. I lower my gaze from his, and I'm confused when I see a miniature Snickers bar.

Is he giving me candy? I don't understand.

"Little Red," he says.

My heart skips several beats, and my entire body starts to tingle all the way down to the tips of my toes. This isn't possible. Right? This can't be the wolf I met at Surrender on Halloween. It can't be. I would have noticed his tattoos. Except he was completely covered from head to toe, and the mask stopped me from getting a good look at his eyes. He even had gloves on. I hadn't seen a glimpse of his skin that night. The wolf had a voice as thick as honey, and he smelled delicious. Fresh, like citrus, but intense at the same time. That was all I'd known about him.

Holy fuck. My eyes widen as the truth crashes through me like a wrecking ball that I wasn't prepared for, and I let out a gasp. "Big bad wolf."

"Aye."

I stare up at him in complete shock. The wolf I'd been dreaming about for months has been right here in front of me all this time, coming into my job every week, knowing who I was when I had no idea who he was. Did he know I'd gotten a job at his pub? I wonder if it was a coincidence that Aiden came into Pete's to offer me a job. Somehow, I know it wasn't.

"I couldn't walk away from you, Little one. I should have, but I couldn't. You got under my skin at Surrender, and I knew the second I saw you I wanted to Daddy you."

This can't be real. I'm dreaming. I have to be. There's no way this is happening. I reach down and pinch my thigh hard, then wince. Declan grabs my hand firmly and narrows his eyes at me. "What are you doing? Don't do that."

His words are sharp, but I'm still sure I'm dreaming so I use my free hand and pinch my other thigh. I let out a hiss of pain this time, and he grabs hold of my other wrist.

"Little girl, I'm going to spank your bottom if you keep doing that."

My eyes snap up to his brooding ones. "I'm dreaming."

He stares at me, clearly confused for several seconds before the realization hits him and he shakes his head. "You're not dreaming, baby. I haven't been able to walk away from you since I met you. I want you, but I can't have you, so I've kept my distance. At least I had until you came to me about your sister."

This time *I'm* confused. "Why can't you have me?"

His thumbs are stroking my wrists now, and my skin buzzes from his touch.

"Because I'm a criminal, and you're a fucking angel. I'm corrupt and you're good. I'm dark and dirty and I'd take over your entire fucking life. You wouldn't ever have a second to breathe with me. You deserve someone better. Someone safe and sane. I'm neither of those things, baby."

There's pain on his face, and I can't resist pulling one of my hands away from his to touch the pinched spot between his eyebrows. He keeps his eyes on mine, and it feels like our souls are connecting and having a conversation with each other.

"I feel safer with you than I've ever felt in my life."

His eyes lower to my mouth for several beats, and I hold my breath waiting for the kiss that never comes. Instead, he steps back and sets the candy bar on the bedside table.

"You are safe with me, Cali. But no matter how many men I have to protect you, there's always danger, and I'm not willing to put you at risk."

I chew on my bottom lip, unsure what to say. His concern means the world to me because deep down I know he's speaking the honest truth. But my heart is hammering in my chest because this man has awakened something inside me. A rush I've never felt before. One I don't want to go away. I want him, and he says he wants me.

"Do I get a say?" I ask.

He looks at me, his hands on his hips and his jaw flexing. "Baby, I would give anything for you to be my Little girl, but putting you at risk isn't acceptable. My job is dangerous, and it's not the type I can just walk away from. It's blood in, blood out. Even when I retire from being the boss, I'll still be in the mafia, and there will still be danger."

"Blood in, blood out" only confirms that he's killed people. It's what he does. He's a criminal, but right now, I don't care. Right now, he's my anchor, and I need him. I want him. I want to call him Daddy, and I want him to possess me in the way he described. No room to breathe. I want it all. Deep down to my bones, I know Declan Gilroy would never harm a hair on my head.

I stand and walk over to where he's standing, looking pained and tense. My eyes are level with his chest, and slowly, I tilt my head back and look at his face. His intense look makes me want to squirm.

"Everything you said, about possessing me, owning me, corrupting me? I want it. Don't let me breathe. I need to know what it's like to feel completely consumed by you," I say with a shaky voice.

When he doesn't reply, I add, "Please, Daddy."

12

DECLAN

Being in control is one of the most important aspects of my job. A leader who isn't in control of their own emotions is dangerous. A risk to everyone. I learned at a young age how to keep myself in check, and I've mastered it over the years. But this tiny Little girl in front of me is making me lose control, and it's fucking terrifying.

Her big brown doe eyes stare up at me, her plump lips are pushed out in a slight pout, and she's wearing her adorable fucking pajamas that are so thin that I can see the outline of her nipples. My fingers ache to touch her, caress her, spank her naughty bottom for testing my control. I'd ruin her. She'll ruin me too. Maybe she already has because I know there's not another woman in this world for me. She's it. But what kind of man am I if I make her mine? She's so good and pure. I'm a monster. I have so much blood on my hands, I could fill a fucking lake with it all. I can't say no to her, though. I have control of everything else in my life, but when it comes to her, I have none. I might dominate her in this relationship, but she'll rule my entire fucking world.

"Do you understand what you're asking, Cali? Do you understand I'd be in charge? I'd be your Daddy, your Dom, your man, and you'd submit completely to me. You'd have rules and boundaries, and you'd be disciplined if you disobeyed me. I'm not an easy man. I'm a rough lover, and I'm filthy as fuck. I'll have you doing dirty shit with me you've probably never dreamed of."

I expect her to back away, shrink down, and tell me to fuck off, but she doesn't. Of course she doesn't. I should know better. My girl is strong. I don't think she's scared of anything. So when she squares her shoulders and smiles, I'm totally and completely fucked.

"I understand, Declan."

We stare at each other for several seconds before I breathe again. "I can't give you forever, baby. I won't tie you to me, to this life. When your sister is back, you and she will return to your normal lives where you'll be safer. Do you understand me?"

Her eyebrows pull together, and I watch her swallow as she blinks several times. She doesn't like what I just told her, but it's for her own good. Once her sister is safe, I'll release her back to her everyday life. I'll make sure both of them are taken care of, but I'll have to live without her. It's the only way to ensure her safety. It's the right thing to do, and as a man whose morals are basically non-existent, I want to do right by her. She deserves it.

Finally, she nods. "I understand."

She doesn't sound as confident as she did a few seconds ago, but I ignore the doubt in her voice as I step forward and wrap my hand around the front of her throat, squeezing the sides of her neck firmly. Her eyes widen slightly, but she doesn't back away or fight me. I move closer until her nipples are brushing against my torso, and the only thing between us is my hand gripping her throat.

"This is your last chance to back out, Cali." I stroke the pulsing vein in her neck with my thumb.

My girl doesn't back down. She looks me right in the eye. "No."

That's all I need to hear before my mouth crashes down on hers. My kiss is rough as I use my tongue to urge her lips apart and let me in. She tastes like heaven, and she kisses me back like her next breath depends on it. I rake my free hand through her hair, fisting the strands to hold her head steady.

A moan escapes as her hands come up to my chest, gripping the opening of my shirt, her fingernails scraping against my chest. My cock is painfully hard. She must feel it against her stomach because she presses her hips against it and makes little mewling noises that turn me completely feral.

I let my hand slide from her throat down the center of her chest until I reach her breasts, and cup one roughly, pinching her pebbled nipple between my thumb and index finger.

Pulling her head back by her hair, I move my mouth to her chin and press kisses to her skin as she pants for air. As I make my way down her throat, I nip, lick, and kiss her while I continue toying with her nipples.

"You're so fucking beautiful. Perfect."

Her fingers slide further into my hair the lower I get, and when I reach the edge of her tank top, I yank it down so fast and hard that one of the straps rips, making her gasp. I cover one of her perfectly pink nipples with my mouth while I cup her other breast. When I sink my teeth into the fleshy underside of her breast, she cries out but doesn't pull away.

"Declan." Her voice is strained and full of arousal, and I fucking love it. I love making her feel as unraveled as I've felt since the night I met her.

"It's Daddy. From now on, you call me Daddy. I don't give a fuck where we are or who we're around, I'm Daddy now. Understand?" I growl before nipping at her breast again.

She cries out but nods at the same time. "Yes! Daddy! Oh!"

Hearing her call me that only spurs me on, and soon, I'm sucking on the delicate skin of her breasts, leaving dark purple marks all over them. I know it's fucked up that it turns me on so much to mark her, but damn, I love it. Mine. She's all mine, and I'm not going to waste a single second of our precious time together. I might not get to keep her forever, but when she returns to her normal life, I want her to know what it feels like to be loved and adored endlessly.

I grip her hips and lift her, moving her to the bed where I push her down to her back with her legs hanging off the edge of the mattress.

"If I touch your pussy, how wet is it going to be for me, Cali?"

A blush rises to her cheeks, and she moves her hands up to her face to cover herself, but my fingers wrap around her wrists and pin them above her head so I can see her beautiful flushed features.

"Don't ever hide from me. I'll spank your ass if I ever catch you hiding from me."

She pulls her bottom lip between her teeth as her entire body trembles beneath me. I can feel the heat of her pussy through our clothes, and I know she's soaked. She really likes the idea of me spanking her ass.

"Are you wet for Daddy, Cali?"

My hands are still pinning hers to the bed, and I'm resting my hips between her parted thighs. She can feel my cock pressing against her core, and it's taking an incredible amount of self-restraint not to rip her clothes off and plunge into her right here and now.

I move one hand so it's gripping both of her wrists as I slide the other down her body. She's trembling beneath me, and her breathing is ragged, but her eyes are sparkling as she keeps them locked on my face. When I reach the hem of her shorts, I tuck my hand into her panties and slowly move lower until I reach between her legs, pleased when I feel nothing but smooth skin.

"Such a good girl keeping your pussy shaved. You'll always keep it smooth for me. If you need help, Daddy would be happy to shave you himself."

"Oh, God," she cries.

"There's no God here, baby. Just you and me. Daddy and baby girl. God isn't going to save you from me."

As I dip my fingers between her lower lips, I groan when I discover just how wet she is. It's like a fucking slip and slide down there and I'm about to have the time of my life at the water park.

"So wet. You're a needy Little girl, aren't you?"

She bobs her head up and down as she chews on her bottom lip, not answering my question. I release her wrists and roughly grab hold of her chin, squeezing slightly until her mouth pops open. Fuck, I want to push my cock in between those plush lips.

"Answer me, Cali. Use your words. Tell Daddy what a needy Little girl you are."

My fingers brush against her clit, and she jolts up, clawing at my chest as she cries out. Holy fuck, she's sensitive. I wonder how long it's been since she's been with a man. Has anyone ever made her come before? Shown her how beautiful and special she is? I absolutely hate the idea of any other man ever touching her, but a woman like her deserves to be shown just how sexy she is. She deserves multiple orgasms, too.

"Please, Daddy. Please! Oh, God! Daddy! Oh!"

I continue rubbing her clit in circles, changing the speed and rhythm, and I can feel her pussy getting wetter and wetter with each passing second.

"Tell me, baby girl, when's the last time a man made you come?"

Her head thrashes from side to side. "Never. I've never... done this."

My fingers still, and her eyes fly open to look at me.

"Why'd you stop?" she asks.

I keep my hand where it is, but I'm completely still. "What do you mean you've never done this?"

She looks nervous as she lowers her eyes from me. "I've never, um, I've never had sex."

My entire body goes rigid. I know I'm glaring at her, but more out of confusion than anger. I see the marks on her breasts and wince. She's never been with anyone. And I'm treating her like a goddamn fuck toy, leaving marks on her. Shit!

I tear my fingers away from her pussy and reach for her top, pulling it up over her breasts before I take a step back. Cali sits up, glaring at me.

"What the hell?" she demands.

Even though I'm kicking myself for what I just did, I can't stop myself from bringing my fingers to my mouth and licking them clean, groaning as I taste her sweet flavor.

"Declan!" she shouts.

I raise my eyebrows and stalk toward her, my hand going to her throat again. "Daddy."

She's not afraid of me. I might look scary as fuck right now, but she's not afraid. She does realize I'm not fucking around, though, because she swallows and murmurs, "Daddy."

"What do you mean you've never been with anyone? You've never had sex?"

When she lowers her eyes from mine, I squeeze the sides of her throat. "Look at me, Little girl. What did I say about hiding from me? Don't hide. Look at me."

I'm pleased when she obeys, though there's something in her eyes I don't like. Shame, maybe?

"I've never been with anyone. I've dated, and I had a

boyfriend in high school, but I've never gone all the way with anyone," she says quietly.

The air is sucked out of my lungs, and I feel like I'm about to pass out. The knowledge that no one has ever touched her makes my possessive side go wild, but I also feel like a dick for being so rough with her. For fuck's sake, she has marks all over her tits. What kind of monster am I? She deserves candles and champagne and flowers for her first time. Someone who can be soft and treat her delicately. I don't think I'm capable of that. There's not a soft bone in my body.

I release her throat, step back, and let out a string of curse words in Gaelic.

"What are you saying? Why did you pull away?" she asks. I hate the insecurity in her voice. I made her feel that way, and I hate myself for it.

"I'm sorry, baby. I was too rough with you. Fuck, I didn't know. I assumed you'd had a Daddy before or boyfriends you'd at least had sex with."

She looks so sad, and it makes my chest ache.

"My boyfriend in high school was my first and only Daddy. He introduced me to the lifestyle, but we never messed around. I've spent time with a Daddy at the club, but he just helped me relax into Little Space. He spanked me over my panties a few times, but we never went any further. I've never trusted anyone enough or liked anyone enough to do more."

The fact that she trusted me and liked me enough makes my ego triple in size, but she deserves better for her first time. I wish I could be soft for her. I wish I was a different person so I could make her mine forever. But I'm not and I can't change.

"I'm going to go run you a bath," I say before walking away, leaving her sitting on the edge of my bed with a sad look on her face that breaks me.

.

13

CALI

What the hell just happened? He left me sitting here with my tank top strap torn, my pussy wet and aching, and hickeys all over my breasts. That bastard. All because I'm a virgin? I thought men liked virgins. Isn't that usually a turn-on for them?

Now, he's in his bathroom, and I can hear the bath water running, but all I can think about is wanting to throttle the stubborn jackass. How dare he leave me like this. After everything he'd said to me. I even called him Daddy. He touched my pussy and licked his fingers. He kissed me like he owned me. And then he just walks away when he finds out I'm a virgin? Uh, no.

My body trembles with a mix of anger and arousal. My pussy is still throbbing with the need for release. No man has ever touched me down there, and when I've done it, it never felt like *that*. How dare he just pull away and leave me hanging?

I look around the room, trying to figure out what to do. I should pack up my belongings and leave. Go back to my apartment and never speak to him again. I need him, though. He's the only person who can help me find my sister. And he promised he wouldn't stop looking until he did. How am I supposed to be around him now? I'm humiliated and pissed. And so fucking turned on, it's painful.

Not wanting to wait until he comes back, I clutch my top to my chest and practically run for my room. As soon as I'm inside, I lock the door behind me, throw myself on the bed, and sob into the pillows. I've never felt so rejected before. I don't even think I felt this rejected by my own father, and he wanted nothing to do with me. Okay, maybe that's not a fair comparison, but the way Declan walked away from me hurts so bad. I want him like I've never wanted a man before, and I practically threw myself at him. He's probably used to it, and that thought makes me even angrier.

"Cali," Declan calls as the doorknob rattles.

I don't answer him. He'll probably unlock the door and let himself in anyway. It's his house, and I'm sure he's not used to being locked out of any room.

"Cali Ann, open the door."

I lift my head and glare. How the hell does he know my middle name? Fuck. I must be totally naïve. He's a mafia boss. He probably knows everything about me. Hell, I'm surprised he didn't get my doctor's records somehow to find out I'm a virgin.

He pounds on the wood. "Open this door right now, Cali."

My anger outweighs my common sense at the moment, so I stomp over to the door, throw it open and glare up at him. "Leave me alone," I snap.

His green eyes seem darker as he glares right back at me. "What did I tell you about hiding from me?" he demands.

I straighten my spine and square my shoulders. I might be a full foot shorter than he is, but I won't let his size intimidate me. I can be a bad bitch. I've done it all my life. I don't need him. Or his massive dick. Even if it *is* something I'll be thinking about for the rest of my life.

"That was before. All of that is null and void now. Go away, *Declan*."

His jaw flexes, and I wonder if it's a good idea to poke the bear, but at this point, I don't care. I know he won't truly harm me. I trust his promise. And I won't be his doormat just because he's a gangster and I'm a poor girl from the wrong part of Seattle.

"Cali," he says in a softer tone. "You deserve more than what I can give you. Your first time should be special and gentle and fuck, it should be with someone you can have a future with."

I'm completely tuning him out. I know I'm being a brat, but I can't seem to stop myself, so I just nod. "Right. Got it. Special, and gentle. Because obviously, I hated how rough you were being. You're really something. You kept a goddamn Snickers bar from Halloween because you said you felt something for me. You came into my job weekly. You dropped everything to help me with my sister. And now you're tucking tail and running because I haven't fucked a football team of guys. So run, Declan. Just run. I'll find someone who will be happy to fuck me when given the opportunity."

His expression turns to pure rage, but before he can respond, I slam the door in his face and lock it. I hate myself for acting so childish, but my pussy is having a temper tantrum, and I'm taking it out on him. I stand at the door, expecting he'll pound on it or come crashing through any second, but after a few minutes pass, I realize he isn't going to. It hurts that he just left without a fight. Why should I expect anything else? We don't know each other. We're strangers. I was just going to be a notch on his bedpost. Even *he* said that once my sister is found, she and I will return to our normal lives. Whatever he and I were going to have wasn't a forever kind of thing. All because he wants to protect me. Ugh. Why does the gangster have to be so sweet?

I go back to the bed, throw myself down face first, and sigh into the pillow. I guess I'll be hiding out in my room for the rest of my stay here. At least it has all the amenities a girl could want. Except for a vibrator. Bummer.

At some point, I doze off to sleep because when I wake, it's to the sound of soft knocking on my door.

"Cali, it's Grady."

Disappointment fills me as I get up. I want Declan to be on the other side of the door. Not Grady.

My tank top falls, revealing one of my boobs. "Oh, hold on!" I call as I rush into the closet.

I find a robe and wrap it around me. The material is so thick and soft, I can't help but smile as I cinch it closed. What must it be like to live in luxury all the time?

When I open the bedroom door, Grady raises an eyebrow at me. "You need to eat lunch. Grace made soup and sandwiches."

"I'm fine, thanks," I reply, keeping my gaze on his shoulder instead of his eyes.

"It's not a request. Boss says you need to eat. We can do it the easy way or the hard way."

My eyes shoot up to Grady's face, and I glare at him. "What do you mean by that?"

The corner of his mouth twitches, and I wonder if he's trying to keep from laughing.

"It means you walk down to the kitchen, or I carry you. Your choice," he responds with a shrug like he didn't just threaten to kidnap me from my room and take me downstairs.

My mouth falls open, and I'm so mad I'm speechless, but I also know Grady isn't giving me an empty threat. If I don't go with him, he *will* pick me up and carry me. Hell, even if I fought him, the man is so large and muscular, I wouldn't stand a chance.

"Where the hell is Declan? He's such a big jerk!"

This time, Grady's smirk turns into a small smile. "Has anyone ever told you when you're mad you're like a tiny fairy having a tantrum?"

Seriously? Did he just call me a fairy? Letting out a huff, I glare at him. "If I were a fairy, I'd use my magic pixie dust to turn you into a toad. A big ugly toad. With a wart."

Grady chuckles in response, which only infuriates me more.

"I'm not hungry," I say as I try to close the door, but he slides his foot against it, stopping me.

"The easy way or the hard way, Cali?" he asks with a smug expression.

I stare up at him in disbelief. This fucker is enjoying himself right now. When he doesn't budge, I let out a huff and motion toward the hall. "Well, let's go then, you big oaf!"

He smiles and steps to the side, but I don't miss the fact that his foot is still just inside my door, keeping me from closing it in his face.

"After you, lass."

I roll my eyes and storm through the threshold. "Always the gentlemen, aren't you, gangster?"

I was trying to insult him, but he just chuckles and says, "Aye."

I'm fuming by the time we get down to the kitchen, and thankfully, Grady doesn't say anything else before he leaves me alone with Grace, who moves about the room, prepping vegetables for what looks like a salad.

"Hi, dear. You missed breakfast this morning. I offered to take some up to you, but Declan suggested you wanted to be alone. You must be starved. I hope you like BLTs and tomato soup."

The older woman's sweetness immediately soothes me,

and I offer her the best smile I can muster. It's not her fault her boss is a big, dumb butthead.

"Thank you, Grace. That sounds delicious."

She lights up with a big smile and starts bustling about to fill a plate for me.

"Would you like to sit in here and eat while I finish the salad for dinner?" Grace asks.

I nod because being around her makes me feel better. Her salt-and-pepper hair pulled up into a neat bun and the soft wrinkles around her eyes from years of smiling make me feel at ease, and I really need that right now.

I pull out a barstool and sit at the enormous island in the middle of the chef's kitchen. It's a kitchen I could only ever dream of having. Everything is clean, the appliances are stainless steel, and the countertops a pristine white marble.

Grace slides a plate, a bowl of tomato soup, and a glass of ice water across to me.

"Thank you, Grace."

"You're welcome, dear. So tell me. What did Declan do to piss you off so badly that you needed some alone time?"

I choke on a bite of sandwich and look up at her.

"You don't work for someone for over twenty years and not see their faults. He's a stubborn one, that boy. Sometimes I want to wring his neck for being such a stubborn pain in the ass," she says.

It takes several drinks of water before I feel like my throat is clear enough to speak. "Why do you work for him, then? Wait, does he force you to? Oh my God, Grace, are you here against your will?"

Grace bursts out laughing. Her shoulders shake from how hard she's giggling, and it makes me giggle too. When she finally gets her composure, she leans her elbows against the counter and looks at me from across the island.

"I'm here of my own free will, Cali. While the man might be stubborn as a goat, he has a good heart, and even though he has a hard job, he always tries to do what's right. Even if he doesn't realize it."

I glance down at my food, ashamed of how I treated him earlier. Even though he left me in the heat of the moment, he did it because he was trying to be a gentleman. He was trying to save my virginity for someone who cares about me. He's always looking out for me, and I wonder just how long he's been doing it. My job? I doubt it's just a coincidence Aiden found me at Pete's. I'm a good server, but I don't know that I'm that good. The security at my apartment? It screams Declan.

"Maybe I overreacted earlier."

Grace reaches across the island and pats the back of my hand. "I doubt it. Besides, Declan needs someone feisty like you to keep him in check. Everyone else just lies down at his feet. I have a feeling you're not that kind of woman, and he needs that. More than he knows. But you didn't hear it from me, dear. Now, eat your food before I have to report back to him with how much you ate."

My mouth drops open as I look up at her. "Will he really ask you that?"

The older woman smiles and winks. "You bet your bippy. He's smitten. I've never seen the man so enthralled."

A soft smile spreads across my face as I nod and pick up my sandwich. "Thanks, Grace. I like talking to you."

"I like talking to you too, Cali. I can already tell Declan is meant to be your Daddy, even if he doesn't realize it."

I start choking again. "Wait, you know about...about that?"

She pats my hand again. "I know everything about Declan and his men. They're all Daddies, Cali. Why do you think they're so damn bossy all the time?"

"I thought being bossy and overbearing was a requirement of being in the mafia," I say with a shrug. "Or that maybe they just had sticks stuck up their butts."

This makes me giggle because it's true, and I'm surprised when Grace starts giggling too. I like this woman. I think we'll be good friends.

Even though part of me is still pissed that Declan got me all worked up only to leave me hanging, another part of me appreciates that he was trying to do right by me in his own way. Even so, I need to keep my distance from him. He doesn't want to get involved with me because I'm a virgin, and the more time I spend with him, the more I'll grow to want him. I don't want to get hurt. I've had enough emotional pain in my life.

14

DECLAN

"Did she come down willingly?"

Grady chuckles as he lowers himself into a chair in my office. "Aye. Begrudgingly but willingly. What'd you do to piss her off?"

I narrow my eyes at him. "What makes you think it was me?"

"Because she was spittin' mad. Like a little pixie just stomping her tiny feet down those stairs. I could see the evil pixie dust shaking off her the whole time. Besides, she's sweet and you're an arse. So, what did you do?"

Grady is one of my best friends. When I was just a boy, I learned that when you found someone loyal, you don't let them go. Grady is one of the most loyal men I've ever known, which is probably the only reason I let him get away with talking to me the way he does.

I sigh and rise from my desk. This conversation is going to require a drink. Or several. Anything to ease my guilt. I walked away from the most beautiful, sweet, delicious-tasting woman, *and* I left her horny and practically panting for me. I truly am an arse.

Once I pour a hefty glass of whiskey for each of us, I sit across from him and take a drink. "She's a virgin."

My friend sits with his elbows on his knees, holding his glass between his legs, and stares at me with a blank expression. "And? That's not an explanation."

I suppose he needs more context, so I spend the next several minutes telling him what happened between us. When I finish, I shake my head, only feeling more pissed at myself than I did five minutes ago.

Killian walks in the door and pauses when he sees us sitting with drinks in our hands. "Am I interrupting?"

Grady snorts. "Aye. You're interrupting our boss telling me what a fucking idiot he is."

Jesus Christ, these men are pains in my ass. Why I ever let them get so comfortable, I have no idea. Sometimes it's great. Other times, they gang up on me like this.

"Aye. Bash told me to avoid Cali for a bit until Declan apologizes for whatever he did to her," Killian replies.

I stand and shake my head. "You fucking bastards. Either help me out here or shut the fuck up and get out of my office."

Grady and Killian burst out laughing, but Killian drops down in the chair I just left.

"Boss, you upset her. You probably embarrassed her and made her feel like you didn't want her," Grady says.

I stop pacing. "Of course I want her. I want her more now than ever. Knowing no man has ever touched her before? That no man has ever touched her body or heard her cry out like I did? Fuck. It makes me feel like I'm losing control with how badly I want it."

Killian scratches his chin. "Maybe you should stop trying to fight it and see where it goes. Wouldn't you rather she lose her virginity to someone like you who will put her needs and pleasure first instead of some fuckboy who only cares about himself?"

The thought of her having sex for the first time with anyone other than me makes me want to kill. "Aye."

Shit. I fucked up. I need to fix this. She needs to understand I only pulled away to protect her. Instead, I ended up hurting her. Relationships have never been anything I've prioritized in my life. Maybe because none of the women I've been with were Cali. None of them felt important like my sweet Little girl.

"I need to go find her," I say before I walk out of my office and leave my men laughing at me.

It takes me a few minutes, but I finally locate her in one of the small living rooms upstairs. Bash is with her, and they're playing some video game together. He's talking shit to her, but she's smiling as her fingers move over the buttons of the controller.

"You're done, Cali. I'm about to kick your ass right now," Bash says.

Cali giggles and shakes her head. "Nuh uh, I'm gonna kick your butt. Stop blocking me! Ugh. Jerk!"

Her enthusiasm is infectious, and the way she's glaring at Bash for beating her makes me chuckle. As soon as she hears me, she turns her head, but her smirk falls, and I can see her shutting down. I hate it.

"Hey, bro," Bash says casually.

"Hey. How was lunch, Cali?" I ask, keeping my gaze on hers.

She gives me a small, polite smile. "Good. Thank you."

I hate the sadness in her eyes. I did that. I hurt her. It's another reminder that it's better if I keep her at arm's length. It's the only way I can protect her from me and this life.

Before I can think of what to say, Killian walks into the room, and I can tell from the expression on his face that something went down.

"What is it?" I snap.

Out of the corner of my eye, I see Cali sit up straight, a

look of fear in her eyes. I want to move to her, pull her into my arms and reassure her, but I don't.

"I got a call from Alessandro De Luca. Vladimir Petrov has been killed," Killian says.

Bash stands, and Grady appears in the room along with Ronan and Keiran. They all stand silently and wait for whatever I'm going to say, but it takes me a moment to process this. I know Vladimir's death has to do with our meeting last night. Which means the person responsible for his death was Ivan. The greedy little fuck is going to cause a war. It was obvious the younger man resented his father for still being in power.

"I want a call with Ivan," I say.

Ronan nods and leaves the room.

"Who is Vladimir?" Cali asks from behind me.

I turn around and look into her wide brown eyes, and I hate that she's so scared right now. When I don't respond right away, Bash steps in for me.

"Ivan's father," he says.

Her gaze snaps to mine, her eyes widening even more. I can't stop myself from going to her. I kneel in front of her and take her shaking hands in mine.

"We're going to find her. I need you to be a good girl and stay here while we do what we need to do. Can you do that, please?"

I hate that her bottom lip trembles, but she nods. "Yes," she whispers.

"I'll meet you guys in my office," I say without removing my gaze from hers.

My men immediately go, leaving just Cali and me in the room. I reach out and cup her chin, pulling her face closer to mine. "I'm sorry, baby girl. I fucked up. I shouldn't have left you like that. I thought I was protecting you, but I hurt you, and I hate myself for doing that. Do you think you can forgive me?"

Her eyes fill with tears, and she nods. "Yes."

She throws her arms around my neck and sobs, and I don't waste a second moving from the floor to the couch so I can pull her onto my lap to comfort her.

"I'm so sorry, baby. I'll make it up to you," I murmur as I stroke her hair.

We sit for several minutes, and when she pulls back, I brush a gentle kiss across her lips. My girl deserves gentle and sweet. I don't know if I'm capable of that, but I'm sure as fuck going to try for her.

"I need to see if Ivan will take my call," I say.

"I know. Can…"

"What, baby? Ask me anything."

She nibbles on her bottom lip. "Can I come with you?"

I'm not sure I want her in on the conversation with Ivan, but I also can't tell her no. She wants to be close to me, and I want that too, so I stand and set her on her feet. "Come on, baby. You can't say a word while I'm talking to Ivan, though. Understand?"

"Yes," she whispers, looking up at me from under her long lashes.

The looks she gives me will be my ultimate doom one day. She breaks down my barriers without even trying.

We go to my office, and I take her hand to tug her toward my desk. Before she can say or do anything, I sit down and pull her onto my lap. When she starts to squirm, I tap on her hip three times. "No," I say firmly but quietly enough that only she can hear.

She looks at me with wide eyes but doesn't say anything and stops wiggling. It pleases me that she understood the warning. I would never discipline her in front of anyone unless it's something we agreed upon, and we haven't gotten to that point yet.

"Good girl," I murmur into her ear.

A shiver runs through her, and I feel it all the way down to my cock.

"Ivan is expecting your call," Ronan says.

I nod. Ronan sets his phone on my desk and puts the call on speaker.

"Not a word, Little one," I whisper.

She nods, and the room is silent as we wait.

"Declan. I take it you heard the terrible news," Ivan says when he answers.

I'm glad we're not on a video call because I can't stop myself from rolling my eyes at the way he's trying to sound distraught.

"I did. I'm so sorry to hear that. This is shocking news to us all, and on behalf of myself and all of my men, we send our condolences," I reply.

Cali stares at me as I talk, and her fingers are fiddling with the buttons on my shirt. I want to comfort her, but I need to stay focused. This jackass is playing a game, and when playing a game, you have to keep your head in it to win.

"Thank you. It's looking like it was a hit from the Italians but I'm still investigating," Ivan says.

I glance at Killian who's shaking his head with disgust. This kid has no idea he just shot himself in the foot even more.

"You let me know what you find out? If it was the Italians, that means they broke the pact."

Ivan clears his throat. "Yes. I'll let you know."

"I know this isn't the best time, but since it seems you're now the one in power, we need to discuss the woman you have. She needs to be released immediately," I say bluntly.

Cali grabs hold of my hand, and I give hers a reassuring squeeze.

"Who is this woman to you?" Ivan asks.

"She's family, which is why you won't hurt a single hair on her head before you release her," I say sharply.

Ivan chuckles. "She's not Irish, Declan. How can she be family?"

Cali's hand squeezes mine as tears gather in her eyes. She stays silent.

"She's my woman's sister. Which means she belongs to me. I'd like to keep the pact, Ivan, but I won't hesitate to end it, either. We don't fuck with each other's families, and we don't deal skin."

It's silent for a long moment as I wait for his response. All of my men are scowling at the phone while tears drip down Cali's face. Killian hands her some tissues before he starts to pace in front of my desk.

"There's no skin being dealt, my friend, and as far as her being family, the pact clearly states in order to start a war under these circumstances, the person must be related by blood or marriage. Neither of those seem to be the case," Ivan says cooly.

Cali lets out a quiet whimper and buries her face against my chest. She's the only thing keeping me from losing my temper right now.

"As far as this missing woman is concerned, it seems as though you have no ground to stand on, Declan. She has no real ties to you," Ivan adds.

I lean forward as much as I can with Cali on my lap, getting as close to the speaker as I can. "Do you want war, Ivan? Do you want the blood of your men on your hands? Because I can promise you, I will tear your organization apart limb by limb, and I will come for you and make you pay for crossing me. Is that really what you want?"

Ivan laughs. It's loud and forced, and I know he's nervous. I can hear it through the phone. He knows how powerful my organization is. I have more men in ranks than any other syndicate in the States. The only group that even comes close to my numbers is the Italians. Alessandro made sure of that. We know there's power in numbers, and between the Irish and the Italians, we outnumber all of the other syndicates put together. Ivan doesn't know the alliance I have with Alessandro, but I can guarantee it will be a painful lesson for him.

"Are you sure you're ready to be the one to break the pact, Declan? Because you know just as well as I do what that means. The implications it will have. Are you ready for that?" Ivan asks.

Before I can respond, the line goes dead.

"Fuck!" Killian shouts so loudly that Cali jumps.

I tighten my hold on her as she looks up at Killian with fear in her eyes. I glare at him.

"Sorry, lass. I just fucking hate that bastard. He killed his own father because he knows if Vladimir had found out, he would have skinned Ivan. This fucking bastard needs to die. I didn't mean to scare you, though, Little one," Killian says.

Cali nods and then turns her attention to me. "What happens now?"

I stroke her back, which helps to soothe the rage boiling inside me. I hope it's helping to soothe her too. "I can't start a war over someone who isn't in the Irish family. It puts my men at risk. Their families. It would be essentially going against my own men by making them go to war for someone unrelated."

I hate my answer. I'm telling her I can't help her, and I've never felt so fucking helpless in my life.

"So if we were married, you could go after him?" she asks.

My hand stills on her back, and I move my gaze to meet hers.

"Yes. He could. If you guys were married, we could do what we need to do to get Scarlet back," Killian says.

Fucking Christ. I'm going to kill my underboss. He's just

looking for a reason to get whacked. I narrow my eyes at him, but the smug smile he gives me tells me he doesn't give a fuck about the threat. He's proud as fuck of himself. I'll deal with him later.

The wheels are turning so loudly inside my girl's head, I can practically hear them squeaking, and I know exactly what she's thinking, but I have to be the asshole who turns her down.

"Baby, we can't get married. Once you're married into the mafia, there is no out but death. There's no such thing as divorce in our world," I say.

Her face drops, and that plush bottom lip of hers trembles. It breaks me inside.

"We'll figure it out. I'm not giving up on getting Scarlet. We will get her back one way or another," I add.

She nods and wiggles off my lap. As soon as we're apart, I feel so fucking empty, and I despise the feeling.

"Can I go take a shower?" she asks quietly.

I want to tell her no. I don't want her to be away from me. I want to take her upstairs to my bathroom, run her a bath, then bathe her with my bare hands and take care of her. Instead of telling her no, I just nod and lift my hand to her chin.

"Go take a shower, baby. I'll come up in a bit," I say before I press a kiss to her forehead.

When she walks out of my office, I turn my attention to Killian, walk over to him, pull my fist back, and slam it into his jaw. He raises his hand to rub the bruise, but he's smiling as blood drips from his mouth.

"You're all fucking meddling assholes. Now she fucking thinks she wants to marry me. Fuck!" I shout.

My anger does nothing to change Killian's expression, and the rest of my men are smirking too. Fucking bastards.

"Maybe you *should* marry her, D. It's obvious you both care about each other. You've cared about her for a long time. For whatever reason, you're being a stubborn arse, and you think by keeping her at a distance, you're protecting her. The best way to protect her is by making her yours," Killian snaps.

He's right. I know he's fucking right, and it pisses me off. If I marry her, I can do what I need to do to save her sister, and I can keep her safe for the rest of her life. I want her to be mine forever, and marriage is one way to ensure she belongs to me. I'm so incredibly fucked in the head, and I know it, but it doesn't stop my smile as I stride out of my office toward the stairs.

15

CALI

I let my tears flow down the shower drain while the water pounds on my skin. It's almost bruising but it feels so good. Declan says he'll find my sister one way or another, but Ivan doesn't seem willing to budge. The only reason I'm not a total hysterical mess is because Ivan implied my sister is alive and he isn't going to sell her. Even though I don't trust anything that bastard says, I'm choosing to believe it because if I don't, I'll crumble, and Declan asked me to be strong. I just don't know how much longer I can be strong.

When the water starts to cool, I turn off the tap and wrap myself in a towel. My skin is bright red from the heat, and my eyes are swollen from crying. I look like a hot mess, but it doesn't matter. My plan is to hide out in my room for as long as I can and lick my wounds.

I pretty much offered to marry Declan, and he turned me down. It shouldn't hurt, but it does. He doesn't want me, and I don't blame him. Honestly, it was selfish of me to even ask him to marry me just so he could start a war to save my sister. A war means blood and death. What kind of person am I to ask Declan to engage his men in that kind of thing on

KATE OLIVER

my behalf? Maybe it makes me a shitty person. Maybe Declan has already corrupted me because I don't care. All I can think about is how badly I want my sister back.

Still wrapped in the towel, I step into the bedroom, only to stop in my tracks when my eyes land on Declan sitting in one of the arm chairs near the fireplace. He's facing me, and his gaze travels over my entire body until he meets my eyes.

"What are you doing in here? You can't just come in whenever you want," I say, bringing my hands up to the closure of the towel to keep it in place.

The corner of his mouth twitches as he raises an eyebrow. "The last time I checked, this was my house, and I can come and go into whatever room I want."

His words are blunt, but his eyes are practically glowing with amusement. He points to the floor between his thighs. "Come here, Cali."

Shit. My knees wobble slightly, and I'm not sure I want to go to him. He's like a drug, and the closer I get, the more I want it. I need to stay far, far away. I also still feel like a complete fool for the whole marriage thing. He probably thinks I'm just some needy woman who wants him for his money and power. God, it's pathetic how I practically threw myself at him.

I glance back toward the bathroom, debating if I want to go back in there and lock the door.

"You run away from me and I'll come after you. I'll break that fucking door down, and then I'll spank your ass for hiding from me after I told you hiding isn't allowed. Now. Come. Here."

His tone leaves no room for argument, and I don't doubt he would spank me if I ran from him. My eyes travel down to his large, tattooed hands. I've only been spanked a few times before, but I have a feeling those spankings would pale in comparison to one from Declan.

I want to be a good girl, though, because that's just who I

am, so I walk slowly toward him. Our eyes stay locked on each other's, and it feels like time stands still, but he doesn't hurry me. He sits silently and waits until I'm standing just in front of him.

"Right here," he says, pointing between his legs again.

He's so bossy, but I love it. It makes me feel taken care of, and I don't have to think so much when he's around because he seems to do it for the both of us.

As soon as I step between his thighs, his hands are on my waist, gripping me tightly. The firm hold is all it takes before I burst out crying again. He doesn't hesitate to lift me and pull me onto his lap even though I'm still damp from the shower and my hair is dripping water onto his shirt.

"That's my girl. Let it all out. Shh. Daddy's got you."

His reassuring words just make me cry harder. I think it's because I feel so safe with him. I trust him to take care of me, so I can let my guard down.

"I miss her so much. She's my best friend," I sob.

I cry for a long time, and he continues to stroke my back and whisper sweet reassuring things to me. When my tears finally stop, I can barely keep my eyes open. When I feel myself being shuffled in Declan's arms, I open my lids and see he's carrying me into the bathroom.

"What are you doing?" I ask.

"I'm taking care of you. Just relax and Daddy will do the rest."

I do as he says and relax against him. When he sets me down on the counter, he stands between my knees with his hands on either side of my hips, his face level with mine. My breath catches in my lungs as I stare at him. He's so beautiful. The sharp line of his jaw, his watery green eyes, those lips that felt like heaven on my skin. He's the definition of gorgeous in every way.

"Declan," I whisper.

"Daddy," he says firmly.

My mind is jumbled, and I so badly want to call him Daddy. I want him to be my Daddy. But what I want and what I need right now are two different things. I want *him*, but I *need* my sister to be rescued.

"If you won't marry me, can I marry one of your men so I'm part of the family?" I blurt.

His eyes darken, and it makes me shiver. Declan is an intimidating man, but right now, he looks terrifying. If I could, I'd shrink away from him, but there's no room for me to move because he's so close to me.

"Over my dead fucking body will you marry another man. Do you understand me? No other man will ever touch you, fuck you, spank you, kiss you, make you scream, or marry you. Do you fucking understand me, Little girl? You. Are. Mine. If I ever hear you talk about marrying another man, I'll put you over my knee, bare your bottom, and spank you with my belt until you're a very sorry Little girl. Are we clear?"

His face is so serious and firm that I swallow hard. He's completely serious and I should be afraid, but instead, my pussy now has a pulse and my bottom is tingling. "Yes."

His nostrils flare. "Yes, Daddy."

"Yes, Daddy," I whisper.

"That's my good girl. You'll marry me. There is no out with us, Cali. Once you're mine, you're mine forever. You will be tied to me and the mafia for the rest of your life. You'll be my queen, but you'll also be my Little girl, and you'll have rules and boundaries. If you disobey or break those rules, you'll be disciplined and treated like a naughty Little girl. I'll suffocate you with my possessiveness. You won't have room to breathe in this relationship. It won't be easy, Cali. I'm not an easy man. I'm demanding and strict and controlling. But you'll want for nothing. You'll be treated like a princess, and I'll take care of your every need, sexual or otherwise. Are you sure you want all of that? You might be marrying me to get your sister back, but you need to be aware of everything that comes along with it."

I'm practically panting. He's telling me all of this as though it's a bad thing. Like I wouldn't want all those things, but I do. I want it all. I want him and I want to be his. I want to belong to him and be his woman and Little girl. I want his dominance and discipline. I need it. I crave it.

"Yes. I'm sure. I do want my sister back. More than anything. But I also want you. I want you to be my Daddy and to give me rules and boundaries, and I want you to make me feel safe and cared for like you already do. I want... I want you to take my virginity and be the only man I ever fuck. I want you to teach me how to please you the way you like so I can make you happy."

He rests his forehead against mine. "You already make me happy, Little one."

We're silent for several minutes until he takes a step back and opens the top drawer of the vanity. He pulls out a wide wooden-backed hairbrush that causes goosebumps to rise over my skin. I know just by looking at it I never want to be spanked by that terrifying object. He sets it on the counter beside me, then picks me up and lowers me to my feet before turning me around so I'm facing the mirror and my bottom is pressed against his front. I let out a soft gasp when I feel the length of his hard cock against me, but he ignores me and starts running the brush through my hair, gently combing through the tangles.

By the time he's done and my hair is shiny and tangle-free, I'm practically a pile of putty. Who knew having someone brush your hair could be so relaxing?

"Let's get you dressed, then we need to go down and meet with my men," he says.

Biting my bottom lip, I look up at him. "Can't we, um, you know? Finish what we started earlier today?"

His cock is still hard, and I can see the outline against his pants. I so badly want to touch it, but he catches my wrist in a firm hold.

"No. If we're going to be married, we're going to do it right, and you're going to be a virgin on our wedding night. I may not be able to do a lot of things right by you, but this is something I can do, so you'll wait."

My shoulders drop. I try to take a step back, but he tightens his hold on my wrist.

"Did you touch your pussy this morning after you ran back in here?" he asks.

I swear my entire face is beet red, so I try to lower it from his so he can't see me, but his free hand catches my chin and forces me to look up at him.

"No hiding from Daddy. That's a rule. Now, did you touch your perfect little pussy earlier?"

Our eyes are locked, and his hand is still holding my chin firmly so I can't look away. "No," I whisper.

The corners of his mouth pull back slightly. "Good girl. Rule number two, you don't touch your pussy without my permission anymore. Not even to tease it. Your pleasure, your orgasms, your pussy, they all belong to me now. Understood?"

My lips part in a soft gasp and my nipples are aching against the soft terrycloth of the towel. I don't know why it turns me on that he's so possessive like this, but I love it more than I could ever explain.

"Yes. I understand."

"Good girl," he says before he yanks the towel away from my body, leaving me completely naked before him.

"I might not fuck you until our wedding night, but that doesn't mean I'm not going to make you scream before then."

Before I can even process what he said, he picks me up and carries me into the bedroom, then lowers me onto the bed. He takes a step back and lets his eyes roam over my body. The way he looks at me makes every bit of insecurity disappear because I can see the approval written all over his face. He moves his hand to his cock and adjusts himself, letting out a low groan.

"Fuck, baby girl. You're going to be the death of me. Spread your legs and show me your pretty pussy," he growls.

My nipples are hard points, and I know my pussy is glistening with my cream. Every nerve in my body is on fire. I've never felt so exposed and vulnerable, but at the same time, I've never felt more beautiful and safe, so I obey him and slowly spread my legs.

His tongue slides over his lips, and he looks like a starved beast. Goosebumps rise all over my body as I watch him move toward me, stalking me. The bed dips from his weight as he puts one of his knees between my legs and hovers over me, his hands coming to rest on either side of my head, his eyes focused on mine.

"You're mine, Cali. I won't let you go, Little girl. I'll own every part of you."

I let out a soft whimper and nod. "Yes, Daddy."

Those two little words set him off, and he goes feral on me, kissing and biting my neck and chest, letting his tongue roam over the marks he left on my breasts, and all I can do is close my eyes and feel every sensation. He sets my body on fire. I want him to own me completely. In every way possible. Hell, I'm pretty sure he already does, and I fucking love it.

He cups my pussy. The contact makes me whimper as his eyes lock with mine.

"This is my pussy now, Cali. It belongs to me. You belong to me."

I bob my head up and down as I try moving my hips to get some pressure right where I need it. Instead of giving me what I want, he lifts his hand and brings it back down, lightly swatting me between my legs.

"Oh!" I cry out, surprised by both the pain and pleasure that swat gives me.

"You needy Little girl trying to seek pleasure without my permission. What am I going to do with you, Cali? Do I need to get a chastity belt and put it on you twenty-four-seven so I know you can't try to pleasure my pussy? Is that what I need to do, baby?"

"No! I'll be good, Daddy. Please. I just…"

He stares down at me, arousal written all over his face, and I can feel his hard length against my thigh.

"I know, baby. You just need Daddy to make you come, don't you?"

"Yes! Please!"

Declan gives me a lazy smile as he cups my pussy again and starts rubbing circles around my clit. "My Little girl has such good manners. I think she deserves a reward."

Oh, thank God. Yes, I definitely deserve a reward.

When he starts kissing my neck, I let my head fall back against the mattress, savoring the sensation of his warm, wet mouth on my skin while he continues to play with my clit like it's his favorite instrument. As soon as he latches his lips around one of my nipples, my body bucks against him, and I'm barely holding on by a string. The urge to come is so strong, yet I feel like I need his permission to let go.

"Daddy, I need…"

He pulls off my nipple with a pop and sinks his teeth into the soft flesh of the underside of my breast before he licks where he just bit.

"You need to come for Daddy, don't you, baby?"

I need it more than I need air right now.

"Yes!"

His fingers start rubbing my clit harder and faster until I'm trembling from head to toe.

"Come for me, Cali."

His permission sets me off, and I scream my release, my

pussy clenching in search of something as he continues to flick my clit and toy with my nipples. Goosebumps rise all over my body, and it feels like my orgasm just keeps coming as he whispers filthy words to me.

"Such a good fucking girl. Goddamn, baby, you're so fucking precious when you come like that."

When my body finally stops convulsing, I'm left panting for air as Declan shifts on the bed and lowers himself between my legs. When his tongue touches my pussy, I jump in surprise and look down at him as he licks me clean, groaning his approval the entire time. Holy hell, he looks so damn sexy as he does it, keeping his eyes locked on mine the entire time.

He licks me for several minutes before he moves up my body, pulling me on top of him and wrapping me in his arms. I feel like I'm home for the first time in my entire life. Right where I'm supposed to be.

16

DECLAN

When her breathing finally returns to normal, I roll her off me and stare down at her sweet face. She's perfect for me in every fucking way, and I can't believe she's going to marry me. Even if it's just to get her sister back, she'll still be mine. I'd prefer she be in love with me, but at least she's comfortable and feels safe around me. And she gets very turned on by me, too. I could spend every night of the rest of my life between her legs, and I don't think I'd ever get my fill. Her cream is like a nectar that will keep me alive.

I have only one hope. That she doesn't start to hate me once she understands the kind of monster I am. I'll do my best to hide my darkness from her, but I won't be able to shield her completely.

"We should go down. I need to put things in motion and warn the other syndicates."

I'd rather stay in bed with her for the rest of the night. I could have Grace bring us dinner so I could feed her without even having to leave the room. I hate that we can't hide in this bubble together. Maybe we're not a real couple, but for the moment, it feels that way, and I don't want it to stop. I've never felt as connected to anyone in my life as I feel with her.

"Okay, I just need to get dressed," she says as she starts to rise from the bed.

I grab her wrist and pull her back down. "Nope. You don't need to do anything besides lie there and let Daddy take care of you."

Her eyes widen. "I can dress myself, Declan."

My girl is going to quickly learn that her obedience is non-negotiable. I move to the edge of the bed and pull her up with me. Before she can move to stand, I wrap my arm around her waist and bring her face down over my lap, making her squeal and kick her feet.

"Declan!"

My palm lands on her ass with a hard, sharp smack. "My name is Daddy. I've told you and reminded you multiple times, so this time, the reminder will hurt."

I smack her ass again, this time the other cheek. I love watching her soft flesh bounce back when I lift my hand. Her round bottom is the perfect fit under my palm, and I have no doubt I'll enjoy spanking my girl often. I've been very lenient with her the past couple of days, but she'll learn quickly that my lenience only goes so far before she'll find herself in this position.

"I'm sorry! I'm not used to calling you Daddy."

She gets another two swats from me and kicks her feet in response. It's adorable. She's my little fighter. I love it.

"I know you're not used to it. That's why this spanking will only be a light one."

Cali huffs. "I don't think this is considered light."

I smile at her sassiness. I'm glad she can't see my face because I don't want her to see my amusement. I spank her several times, a bit harder, alternating cheeks. Every time she kicks her feet, I catch glimpses of her pussy and the fresh arousal coating her bare lips. Her ass might be stinging, but she doesn't hate it.

"I can make it harder if you want to keep sassing me, Little girl. You're going to learn who the boss is in this relationship. You want a Daddy, and I'm the Daddy. I'll be your man and your husband, but above all of that, I'll be your Daddy, and you will follow the rules or you will be punished. Are we clear on that?"

She lets out a whimper as she squirms against my tight hold. She's not ready to stop fighting me yet, and that's okay. I'll sit here all day staring at her pink ass and wet pussy while spanking her until she decides to be a good girl.

"Since I have you here with your undivided attention, I think it's a good time to start giving you rules. First rule, my name is Daddy to you. You call me Daddy at all times. I don't care where we are, who we're around, you call me Daddy unless it's a hard limit for you. Is it a hard limit, Cali?"

I pause the spanking to give her a second to think about that. Even though I want her to call me Daddy at all times, if she tells me it's a hard limit, I will respect that. I might be her Daddy, but she still gets a say.

"No," she finally says.

A triumphant smile crosses my face, and I start spanking her again, working my hand all over her bottom and the tops of her thighs.

"Ouchie!" she whines.

"Good. That was rule number one. Rule number two, no hiding from me. That means physically and emotionally. You don't hide your body, your mind, or your heart. If you want to say something, you say it. Don't hide. If you're embarrassed, you don't move away from me to hide it. I want all of you, Cali, and I won't allow you to hide any part of yourself from me. Are we clear on that?"

She whimpers her agreement as she scissors her thighs,

looking for some friction on her swollen pussy. This spanking isn't for her pleasure, though, so I slap the backs of each thigh sharply. "Spread your legs."

I'm pleased when she obeys, even though she lets out a sad little sound of protest. She's so fucking expressive.

"Rule number three, we already talked about. No touching or playing with your pussy. The only time you're allowed to touch your pussy is for hygiene purposes. If I catch you playing with your pussy or giving yourself orgasms without my permission, I'll edge you for hours and then spank your ass until you're a very sorry Little girl. Understand?"

"Yes," she cries out, kicking her feet again.

"Good girl. Do you know what a safeword is, Cali?" I pause because I want to make sure this part of our conversation is crystal clear to her.

"Yes."

"Good. Your safeword is red. Is that easy enough to remember?"

She nods. "Yes."

"Okay. If at any time you need something that's happening between us to stop, you say that word and everything stops. I expect you to use your safeword if you need to. It's there for a reason, and that reason is so you feel safe. You're always safe with me, but sometimes things can feel too intense and scary, and it's okay if you need things to stop. Even when you're being punished. Understand?"

She twists to look back at me, meeting my gaze. I pin her with my eyes and wait for her to answer.

"I understand. Thank you," she says softly.

I lift my hand and stroke her hair. "I know you haven't always felt safe, Cali. That changes with me. You're always safe with me. The rest of the world gets a different side of me. They aren't safe from me. You are. Always."

She nods. "I'm sorry I didn't call you Daddy."

Fuck. She melts me like butter. My hard shell is softening each minute I'm around her. "Thank you for apologizing. We're not done, though."

The noise of protest she lets out makes me chuckle as I start spanking her again. It's not a very hard spanking. I'm mostly trying to get a gauge on her pain threshold so in the future I don't push her too hard or far. I never want to hurt her, so I need to learn where her limits lie.

"Rule number four, you don't ever, *ever*, go anywhere without my men with you. Your life is going to change drastically, Cali. You will have guards with you everywhere you go. You will be protected and watched all the time. You will obey my men when they give you a safety rule. This is a very serious rule. I will not take your punishment lightly if you break this rule. Your safety is the most important thing to me." I give her an extra hard spank on each cheek to drive home the point, and with each swat, she cries out loudly. "Are we crystal clear on that rule, Cali Ann?"

I'm surprised when I hear her sniffle. "Yes."

Her voice is trembling, and it tugs at my heartstrings. My girl might be tough but she's also fragile, and I suspect the responsibility for her safety has always fallen on her shoulders. That ends now.

"Rule five, you come to me for everything. I don't care where I am, what I'm doing, or who I'm with, you find me, call me, whatever, and ask for what you want or need. I'll never be too busy for you. If for some reason you can't reach me, go to Killian. Understand?"

"Yes."

I'm not even spanking her now. She's relaxed over my lap, and I have one arm holding her in place while my other hand rests on her bottom. Her flesh is warm under my touch. Not warm enough, though, so I raise my palm and bring it down with a sharp smack that makes her cry out.

"Rule number six, I pick your outfits and get you dressed

each day. If for some reason I'm not here to get you dressed, I'll tell you what to wear. You're not allowed to dress or undress yourself anymore. Unless I get you dressed in the morning, you stay in your pajamas until I do. Same with your hair. I will brush your hair each morning and night and put it in pigtails or a ponytail. Any questions about that?"

She peers back at me again as though she isn't quite sure if I'm being serious or not, so I give her a stern look that expresses just how serious I am.

"I can dress myself," she murmurs.

I give her bottom several smacks. "I don't doubt it, but you're no longer allowed to do that. It's Daddy's job now. It's a rule, and if you break it, you'll be punished. Got it?"

"Yes. Owwie!"

I continue to spank her for several minutes, and when I hear her sniffle again, I stop and pull her up to sit on my lap. Tears roll down her cheeks. She snuggles into me, her naked body fitting against my chest perfectly, and I realize right then and there she is exactly where she's meant to be—and so am I. She probably doesn't realize it yet, but she owns me just as much as I own her. Maybe even a little more.

17

CALI

As we make our way downstairs toward his office, I'm nervous. Will his men think badly of me for wanting to marry Declan so he can start a war? I know it's selfish, but I'm desperate to find my sister. I can't live without her in my life. She's my best friend in the whole world, and I feel so empty without her. I want to tell her all about Declan and the dirty details of what he did to me earlier.

I'm wearing a pair of hot pink leggings and an oversized knit sweater that nearly comes down to my knees. Declan picked my outfit and dressed me like I was a helpless Little girl, and though it was slightly embarrassing at first, I secretly loved every second of it. I'd been a little surprised when he'd chosen a pair of my plain cotton panties over a sexier pair. Not that I mind. I prefer wearing cotton briefs over uncomfortable, sexy panties because they make me feel innocent and small.

"I'm scared," I say as we step off the last stair.

Declan stops and turns toward me, keeping his hand clasped with mine. "Why?"

I stare at the buttons of his black shirt until he takes my

chin between his fingers and tilts my head back. His green eyes burn into me, and I know deep within my soul I'm going to fall hard for this man. Maybe I already have.

"They might hate me for asking you to start a war."

He takes a step closer to me until his mouth hovers just above mine. "My men care about you. They care about Scarlet too. What Ivan is doing isn't right, and while he may not be directly going against the pact, he's headed in that direction. A war will come either way, the only difference is how soon."

Before I can respond, he presses his lips to mine and kisses me deeply, moving his hand from my chin to the back of my neck, squeezing the sides firmly as he nudges my mouth open with his tongue. I comply and kiss him back, my hands sliding up his hard chest. I'm dying to see his naked body. I've only caught glimpses and feels, and I want more. I want to feel his cock inside me. I want him to hurt me as he fucks me and takes my virginity. He thinks I need soft and sweet, but he doesn't know I don't want that. I've never wanted it. I've always wanted hard and all consuming. Declan is the exact type of Daddy I've always fantasized about. Well, not the gangster part but everything else.

When he pulls his mouth away, I let out a soft whimper of protest and stick my bottom lip out in a slight pout. He smirks at me and leans down so his lips are near my ear.

"You're such a naughty girl. I can hardly wait for the day when I'll get to sink my cock into you and turn you into my dirty Little girl. Daddy's going to fuck you so good in all three of your precious holes. I'm going to own every inch of your body. Now, put that lip away before I force you to your knees and feed you my cock."

He pulls away as a tremble shakes my body all the way down to my toes. My knees are shaking, and I'm not sure I can walk right now. He talks so filthy and knows exactly what to say to make my pussy throb with arousal. God, I want him to force me to my knees. I want him to fuck my mouth the way I've read about in books. It sounds so incredibly hot, and I have no doubt I'll love sucking him.

The sound of his chuckle makes me glance up at him. "You like the sound of that, don't you, Little girl?"

I take an unsteady breath and give him a slight nod. "Yes, Daddy."

A low growl rumbles up from his chest. "Fuck. You're so fucking perfect for me. Come on, we need to get this meeting over with so we can eat dinner and go back upstairs. I'm moving you into my room tonight so I can tongue fuck your pussy any time I want from now on."

He tugs me away from the stairs. I almost trip because of how wobbly my legs are, but he catches me and steadies me with his arm around my waist. I sigh with pleasure at the strength of this man. He overpowers me, but he uses that power to protect me instead of harm me.

Killian, Bash, Grady, Ronan, and Keiran are all there and don't seem surprised when we come through the door together. My cheeks heat as their gazes land on us. I wonder if they can tell what went on upstairs. I fight the urge to reach back and rub my still stinging bottom. Declan told me rubbing wasn't allowed after a spanking, which I think is super mean, but I'm not about to test that rule.

"Feeling better after your shower, lass?" Bash asks with a smirk.

Killian smacks Bash upside the head as my cheeks get even hotter. I step closer to Declan to try to hide my embarrassment. Thankfully, he pulls me against him protectively and leads me behind his desk where he sits down and pulls me onto his lap. I don't squirm this time. I like being perched here. I feel safe and cherished and special. No one has ever made me feel as special as Declan does. He might think he's a monster but to me, he's anything but.

"We're getting married," Declan announces.

My eyes widen as I look around the room, expecting the men to be pissed or disgusted or shocked, but I don't see any of that. Instead, they're all grinning at Declan. Bash does a fist pump while Killian gets up from his seat and walks over to shake Declan's hand. As Killian gets closer, I notice a fresh cut on his lip. I wonder how that happened, but I don't say anything. My tummy churns with nerves. Declan must sense it because he gives me a reassuring squeeze.

"Glad to have you a part of our family, lass," Killian says with a wink.

"Thank you."

Once Killian sits back down, the room goes silent, and all eyes go to Declan, but before he says anything, I blurt, "I don't want you guys to start a war if you don't have to. Can we try to get him to release Scarlet willingly first since she really will be in the family?"

When I finish, I realize what I just did and how disrespectful it was of me to speak before Declan had a chance.

I turn back toward him. "I'm sorry," I whisper.

Instead of being angry, he smiles at me and presses a kiss to my temple. "You heard her. Let's try to do this the nonviolent way first. If he won't cooperate, though, we do what we have to do to get Scarlet back and eliminate Ivan and his whole crew."

And just like that, the men agree, and they start talking about their plan of action to get things rolling. Meanwhile, I sit on Declan's lap and listen while soaking in the feel of his hand stroking my thigh. It's like he's grounding me in a way.

"Baby girl," he says, breaking me out of my thoughts. "I want you to go eat. Grace has dinner ready. I'll be there in just a few minutes."

"I can wait for you."

Three taps on my bottom is all it takes for me to understand it wasn't a request, and I need to obey, so I rise from his lap, but stop when his hand wraps around my wrist. I turn and look back at him.

"Kiss me," he says.

I shift and glance nervously around the room at the five other men. Declan squeezes my wrist, making me look back at him. His eyes are sparkling as he tugs me toward him. He uses his free hand to capture my chin, pulling my face toward his. I like when he maneuvers me like this because while my mind is racing with insecurities about kissing him in front of his men, he just makes it happen so I can't think too much about it.

My lips land on his. It's not just a peck. He kisses me deeply, holding my chin tightly so I won't be able to pull away until he's ready. When he uses his tongue to part my lips, I give in to the kiss, melting against his touch. It's like he puts me under his spell every time he touches me.

When he releases me, I'm practically panting, and he has a hint of a smile on his lips.

"Go eat, Little girl. I'll be there soon."

I nod and hope Declan's men don't see how wobbly I am as I head toward the kitchen, passing several guards on the way who only give me a single nod of acknowledgment. I don't really know any of their names yet, and they aren't as friendly as Declan's closest men, but I feel safe around them. I guess that's all that matters.

Grace is in the kitchen humming some song, and as soon as she sees me, she grins. "There's the girl who's going to make Declan Gilroy the happiest man in the world. Have you thought about what kind of dress you want, dear?"

I pause mid-step. "How do you already know?"

The older woman chuckles. "Word travels fast around here. Declan likes everyone to know what's going on so we can be prepared for anything that comes our way. This is the best news I've heard in a long time."

She wraps me up in a hug, and I let out a breath I didn't

know I was holding. Being hugged by an older woman isn't something I'm used to. My mom never hugged us. Somehow, being wrapped up in Grace's arms is what I'd imagine it would feel like to be hugged by a mom.

When she releases me, she holds me at arm's length as she smiles warmly. "You're going to make the most perfect bride."

I shake my head. "It's not going to be like an actual wedding."

Grace just shrugs and smiles. "We'll see. It might not be a huge event, but I know Declan, and I see his feelings toward you. He's going to make it as special as he can for you."

I'm not sure what to say to that. I know Declan likes me. His cock has been hard every time I brush against his groin, so obviously he's attracted to me. But I wonder if he likes me in more than just a physical way. I've never felt like a very lovable person. I'm sassy and awkward. The only person who has ever truly loved me is my sister.

Bash walks in and plucks a tomato out of the large salad bowl. Grace glares at him as he pops it into his mouth, but he returns her glare with the million dollar smile that would melt just about any woman alive no matter their age. I can't deny that Bash is gorgeous, but to me, he doesn't compare to Declan.

"You need to eat. If Declan comes in here and you're not eating, he's going to redden your bottom," Bash says.

My eyes widen and my cheeks heat, but Bash just chuckles and slings an arm around my shoulders. "Don't worry, Little one. We're all Daddies. We know what happens when Little girls like you disobey."

Why can't the floor open up and swallow me right about now?

Grace is busy making a plate of food, and once it's filled, she holds it out for me. "Here. Sit and start eating. Bash is right. He will redden your butt if you're not eating when he told you to."

Okay, now I really want the ground to swallow me up, but neither of them seem to be the least bit shy about the topic. Bash leads me to the kitchen island and takes my plate from me, setting it on the counter. "Sit. Eat."

I let out a shaky sigh and climb onto one of the available barstools. Bash leans his hip against the counter, watching me curiously. Does he think I'm only marrying his brother to use him? In a way, it *is* what I'm doing, but I really like Declan, and I don't think I'll mind being tied to him for the rest of my life. But I do need to know if Bash and the others think terribly of me. Even though I don't know Declan's men very well, I like and respect them, and it's obvious they care about their boss.

"Do you guys all hate me?" I finally ask.

Bash's eyebrows pull together in confusion. "Where did that come from, lass?"

"Because I asked Declan to marry me? I don't want you to have to go to war. I understand if you hate me. I just, please don't be upset with Declan. I don't want you to resent him for something I asked for. I just, I miss my sister so much and I want her back and…"

I have to stop talking because the lump forming in my throat feels like the size of a baseball, and tears are threatening to fall. Bash sits on the stool next to me and turns me so I'm facing him instead of the counter. He grabs my chin roughly so I'm forced to focus on his deep green eyes. In a lot of ways, he looks just like Declan, but their eyes are complete opposite. Declan's are light pools of green, and Bash's are a deep emerald that darken when he's pissed. Right now, they're almost black.

"I'm only going to say this once, lass, so listen up. None of us hate you. We're fucking stoked that my brother finally pulled his head out of his ass. We've known you were his for months. When he claimed you as his, you became our family too. The mafia might define it as marriage or blood, but we don't. You're our family, and so is Scarlet. You make my brother happy, and it's pretty obvious to us that you care about him. You might be rushing into this marriage so we can save your sister, but it would have happened eventually anyway, so why wait?"

A tear rolls down my cheek, and I can't stop myself from throwing my arms around Bash's waist. He immediately wraps me in an embrace and kisses the top of my head. "Don't worry, lass. We're going to get your sister back."

Those words of reassurance make me feel better, and I think Bash is quickly becoming one of my favorite people after Scarlet and Declan. He's a smart ass, but I think deep down, he has a really big heart.

"Why are you all over my girl?" Declan growls.

I startle at the sound of his voice and turn, swallowing thickly at the rage in his eyes. As soon as he sees my face, though, his anger turns to concern, and he rushes for me, picking me up and setting me on the counter, wedging himself between my knees.

"What's wrong, baby girl? Why are you crying? What did Bash do to you? You want me to kill him?"

He uses his thumbs to wipe away my falling tears, and it's like he sees no one else in the room besides me. I can't help but smile at his offer to kill his own brother. I know he's not serious, but it's cute he offered.

"Your Little girl is worrying we might hate her. I was reassuring her. Shit. Are you going to go all grizzly every time I hug or touch her? She's about to become my little sister," Bash says.

I giggle and glance at Bash and then back at Declan. "Can we feed him to the fishies?"

Declan stares at me in shock for a couple of seconds and then bursts out laughing while Bash narrows his eyes at me.

"What the hell? I thought we were friends, brat," Bash says, though I can tell he's fighting a grin.

"Baby girl, you have got to stop reading those fucking mafia books."

I shrug. "I have to learn the business somehow, don't I? If I don't read those books, I won't know which finger to cut off or what river to throw the bodies in."

Both Declan and Bash stare at me in complete shock, which makes me burst out laughing. The two men look at each other and then back at me again.

"Rule number seven, no more mafia books or movies," Declan says.

"We'll see about that," I reply.

Bash lets out a low whistle as he makes his way toward the kitchen door. "Good luck with that one, brother. I have a feeling she's going to run circles around you."

Declan's leans closer. "You're just dying to get your ass *really* spanked, aren't you?"

I shake my head and bite my lower lip, not wanting to dig myself any deeper into my hole. My bottom is still tingling from the spanking earlier.

He smirks and lifts me down from the counter. "You haven't eaten like I told you to. I think before bed tonight, you're going to spend some more time over my lap while we have a talk about obedience."

Oh, super. My bottom clenches at the thought. I have a feeling a lot of our conversations will happen with me bent over his lap. The thought doesn't sway me, though. In fact, it makes me want him to be my Daddy even more. I just hope I can be the woman and Little girl he needs in his life. I hope I can be enough for him.

18

DECLAN

When I saw Bash's arms around Cali, I felt so much rage at another man touching my woman that it scared me a little. Bash is my brother. He would never betray me. The rational side of me knows that. The possessive and jealous side of me was ready to rip him to shreds without a second thought. I felt like a complete asshole when I found out he was hugging her to comfort her. I'm going to need to rein myself in, though. Cali will be constantly surrounded by my men, and if I'm not there to give her the comfort she needs in the moment, I want them to be there for her just like I would do for them.

"Sit down. I'm going to feed you. I'm starting to think I'm going to have to feed you every meal to make sure you eat."

Her cheeks turn pink, and there's a ghost of a smile on her lips that tells me she doesn't hate the idea. I don't hate it either. If it were up to me, I would be with her from the time she wakes up to the time she goes to bed, taking care of her, feeding her, dressing her, bathing her. I know I have a job to do, and I'll continue with that aspect of my life, but whenever I'm around Cali, the monster inside of me is quiet.

Maybe that's why I fell for her the night I met her at Surrender. The moment I saw her, everything ugly inside of me quieted. I hadn't ever experienced that before.

I start to feed her bites of steak, salad, and cubed potatoes, and I'm happy she's eating something.

"You need to eat too," she mumbles after swallowing a bite.

"Are you trying to top me, Little girl?"

Her eyes widen and it makes me grin. When she sees me smile and realizes I'm just teasing her, she sticks her tongue out at me.

"Maybe I need to feed *you* to the fishies, Daddy."

I freeze, my hand mid-air, holding a fork with a piece of steak speared on it. This is the first time she's called me Daddy without me prompting her, and it feels like I just won the goddamn lottery. I don't even mind that she just talked about feeding me to the fish. Although I really do need to find her mafia books and get rid of them.

"Say that again, baby."

"What? Daddy?"

"Yeah. I like hearing that from you."

She smiles and lowers her gaze from mine. "I like it too," she whispers.

I've fucked up a lot of things in my life. I've made bad decisions. I've hurt people. I've tortured people. I've killed people. But the one thing I can say for sure is that I will never hurt this woman. I won't fuck this up. It's precious in a way most people would never understand. I do, though. I know how special this is.

"I'm full," she finally says.

I drop the fork, causing it to clatter against the plate, and pluck her from the stool. "Good because I want to give you a bath and take you to bed."

She giggles. "I already took a shower."

"Even better. Straight to bed. It's my turn to eat now. I'm fucking starving."

Instead of taking her to her bedroom, I carry her into mine. She won't be returning to that room again.

When I set her down on the edge of my bed, I hover over her, not giving her an inch of space. I want to be as close to her as I can and drink in her scent. She smells like vanilla and cherries. I just realized cherries are now my favorite food.

Even though I'm the one who dressed her, I'm irritated with the amount of clothes she has on, so I start to pull them from her body as if she's a rag doll I'm undressing. She lets me without a fight, and while I love the fire she has inside her, I also love that she's such a good girl in the bedroom. I'd much rather give her good girl spankings instead of having to discipline her.

"I want to see you." Her bottom lip is pushed out in a pout as her eyes roam over my button-down shirt and slacks.

Until this point, she hasn't seen more than a little bit of my chest and my forearms. She hasn't seen my scars. Bullet wounds and knife wounds. She has no idea how many times I've come close to death. I don't want her to know. I want her to live in blissful ignorance, but I can't hide from her. She's not allowed to hide from me so it wouldn't be fair. I start opening my shirt, loving the way her eyes travel lower with each button I undo.

When I reach the last one and pull my shirt away, her mouth falls open as she takes me in.

"You have so many tattoos," she murmurs.

I take a step closer. She still has her bra and leggings on, and it's still far too many clothes for my liking, so I wrap my hand around her slender wrist and pull her to stand. I keep my eyes locked on hers as I yank her leggings down, then kneel in front of her so she can step out of them.

Fuck, she's so beautiful. Every curve of her body is like an adventure I can hardly wait to explore. I can't believe she's a virgin, and she's going to belong to me and only me.

Her breath hitches when I rise so her lace-covered breasts are pressed against me. I move my hand to her throat, squeezing the sides firmly, loving the little moan she makes as I rub my thumb over her racing pulse.

When her hand slides between us, toward my cock, I grab her wrist and twist it behind her back. "No touching," I growl into her ear.

She lets out a frustrated sound. "I want to touch you, and... and I want to see you and taste you like you did for me."

Goddamn. I thought I'd learned control when I was younger, but now I'm realizing no matter how much I've practiced it, this Little minx is always going to test me. And today, I'm going to fail because there's no fucking way I can say no to her lips wrapped around my cock.

I lower my face and brush my lips over hers. "You want to suck Daddy's cock?"

She nods. "Uh, huh."

"Ask nicely. Little girls who don't use their manners don't get what they want."

Another frustrated sound escapes, and I feel her flex the hand that I'm still holding behind her back. She looks up at me, her tongue darting out to wet her plump lips. Her cheeks are flushed, but I can still see the determination in her eyes, and it turns me on. My girl might be nervous, but she's tough, and she's not going to back down from a challenge.

"May I taste your...your cock?"

I smile and take it a step further. "Please, Daddy."

Her eyes narrow and she shifts slightly. "Please, Daddy?" she repeats.

"You're such a good girl. Yes, you may taste my cock, baby. Are you sure you're ready for that?"

"Yes."

I'm surprised how sure she seems about it, especially since she's never messed around with a guy, but I'm not going to question it. My beautiful girl is asking to suck my cock. I release her hand and take a step back to remove my pants and underwear. Her eyes follow my every move, and when I kick off my shoes and drop my slacks, her eyes widen as she takes in the outline of my cock through my boxer briefs.

"It's, uh," her tongue darts out to lick her lips, "so big."

She's practically panting the words, and when I hook my thumbs into the waistband of my underwear and pull them down, letting my cock spring free, her eyes nearly pop out of her head.

"Come here, Cali."

When she takes a step forward, I give her a slight nod. As soon as she gets close to me, I grab her wrists and yank until she crashes into my chest.

"You're going to be a good girl and do what Daddy says. If you need to stop at any time and you can't speak, you tap my thigh three times. Understood?"

Her pupils dilate as she nods, her mouth hanging open. Fuck, I know I'm going to come embarrassingly fast, but I can't seem to find it inside myself to care.

"On your knees, Cali."

I release her wrists and wait for her to obey my command. Her throat bobs as she swallows heavily before she sinks to her knees in front of me. As she looks up at me with her sparkling brown eyes and her lips slightly apart, I realize I'm the luckiest man in the entire world. She was made for me, and I almost hate myself for telling her we're going to wait until our wedding night to fuck because all I can think about is plunging into her tight little pussy.

"Open your mouth, Little girl. What are you going to do if you need me to stop and you can't speak?"

She looks slightly surprised by the question but she quickly answers. "Tap on your thigh three times."

"That's my good girl. Daddy's going to fuck your beautiful mouth, and when I come, you're going to swallow every drop. Understood?"

19

CALI

Oh my God.

This man drives me wild. He's so demanding but with every command, he turns me on more. My panties are soaked through. If I didn't have them on, I'm pretty sure I'd be dripping onto his plush carpet. I'm dying to touch myself but he hasn't given me permission. I don't want to do anything that will get me in trouble. I don't want to lose my chance to suck his beautiful cock.

I've watched a lot of porn over the years, but I've never seen a cock so perfect. It's long and thick, with rigid veins and a thick mushroom head. I have no doubt it's going to be painful when he takes my virginity, but I also can't wait to feel that pain. The man will probably split me in half, but that only turns me on even more.

"Cali. Daddy asked you a question."

Shoot. What was the question? Oh, right. Swallow. I nod. "Yes, Daddy."

His gaze stays on me for a long moment before he slides his fingers through my hair and starts to guide my mouth toward his cock.

I smooth my hand over the length of it, and just that

small touch makes him groan. "Fuck, baby. You have about thirty seconds to explore my cock with your hands and your tongue and then Daddy's going to fuck your mouth until I come down your throat."

He releases my hair, his hands flexing at his sides as though he's struggling to keep control. That only spurs my arousal. I love seeing him like this.

Using the tip of my index finger, I follow one of the veins on his cock before I wrap my hand around it, smiling when it twitches in my palm. I'm intimidated by his size, but I've watched enough dirty movies to have an idea what to do, so I lean forward and kiss the tip of his cock before swirling my tongue around the head. Declan hisses, and his head rolls back for a second before he looks down at me again, our eyes locked on each other.

I open my mouth wider and take in as much of his length as I can until it reaches the back of my throat, and I gag slightly.

"Fuck, baby. I love that sound. So beautiful."

His praise is all I need to hear to do it again, gagging before pulling back to take a breath.

When I close my lips around him and suck, he groans and moves his hands back to my hair, taking fistfuls of my locks in his fingers. "Your time is up, Little girl. Daddy's going to fuck that pretty little mouth now. Hands on my thighs."

I move my hands to his powerful thighs and relax my jaw as much as I can. His grip is firm, and the slight tug of pain only turns me on more as he guides me how he wants before he starts thrusting in and out of my mouth. He goes slow and shallow at first, and I let out a moan as the head of his cock reaches the back of my throat, cutting off my air for just a second before he pulls back.

Before long, his thrusts become more rapid, going deeper and deeper until I'm gasping for air whenever I can, but I don't want him to stop or slow down. My pussy is loving every second of this, and I'm loving how out of control he is as he starts panting and cursing under his breath.

"I'm going to come, baby, and you're going to swallow every drop," he growls.

The tight hold he has on me makes it so I can barely nod as I hold on for the ride. His eyes go wild and his deep thrusts suddenly turn erratic. He holds my head still as his cock starts pulsing, pushing out hot come into the back of my throat.

I swallow as much as I can, but there's more than I expect and a few drops leak out of the corners of my mouth and down my chin. Declan pulls himself free and stares down at me as he uses his index finger to swipe the semen from my chin before he slides the digit into my mouth.

"Suck it clean," he orders.

I swirl my tongue around his finger and hum my appreciation for his flavor as I look up at him from under my lashes.

"Fuck. You're perfect for me, baby. So fucking sexy and naughty," he murmurs as he pulls his finger free.

Without warning, he pushes me onto the mattress and prowls toward me on the bed like a panther ready to attack.

"Spread your legs and show me my pussy. I'm fucking starving."

He doesn't have to ask me twice. As soon as I do as he says, his mouth is on me, licking and sucking my clit, giving me no mercy as he takes what he wants and his hands roam my body.

When he inserts a single finger into my pussy, I cry out and wiggle my hips to try to get used to the sensation. I've never played with myself like this, so the feeling is foreign and a little uncomfortable at first but then he curls his finger and sucks on my clit at the same time. Before I can ask permission to come, I explode so hard I'm practically seeing stars.

My orgasm comes in waves, and he continues to lick, suck, and finger fuck me through it all until I'm a whimpering pile of goo on the mattress.

Declan slowly pulls his finger from me and sucks it clean before he moves up the bed and wraps me in his arms, cuddling me tightly against him as we come down from our highs together.

20

DECLAN

I'm in love with her. Maybe I have been for months. Without a doubt, she's the one I will love for the rest of my life.

As she snuggles in deeper against my body, I wrap my arm around her and nuzzle her neck. She's soft and feminine, but she's so fucking strong and resilient. It makes me love her even more. She'll never be a doormat, and she'll always challenge me. I need that. She'll keep me grounded and keep my ego in check. I want to make her the happiest woman in the world because she's already made me the happiest man. She may not be marrying me for love, but she *is* marrying me, and I hope one day she'll fall head over heels in love with me. Finding and saving her sister is the first step in the right direction.

"Tell me about Scarlet."

She tenses for a second before she lets out a soft sigh and burrows even closer to me. "We've always been close. We had to be. Our dad wanted nothing to do with us, and our mom was too busy drinking and doing drugs to be a mom."

I stroke her arm. "So you had to be responsible for both you and Scarlet."

"Yeah. Scarlet has always been a little more carefree. A little wild. But we balanced each other out. She never let me be too serious, and I always looked out for her. We take care of each other in our own ways. I guess I didn't do a very good job."

"You're not to blame for this, Cali. She's not either. The only person to blame is that fucking prick."

She sniffles and it breaks my heart. I want to kill that bastard with my bare hands for making my girl sad.

"I miss our movie nights together. I miss everything about her."

Even though I don't know her sister, Scarlet will be a major part of my life since they're so close. My girl loves her sister so much, and I love her too. Scarlet is a part of my family now, and I feel a swell of emotion inside me over the fact that she's not here.

"What movies do you two watch?"

Cali lets out a soft giggle. "*Beauty and the Beast* is our favorite. We drink cheap wine out of cute glasses and eat Cheetos and chocolate and gummy candies and whatever junk food we have in the apartment. We always talk through whatever movie we're watching, but that's when we share all of our best secrets. I miss it so much. I miss her so much."

She sniffles again and raises her hand to her face to wipe the tears from her cheeks. I lean over and kiss her temple and use my thumb to dash away her remaining tears.

"We'll get her back, baby. Ivan and his men will pay dearly for what they've done. I'll avenge you and your sister. I promise you that."

When she doesn't respond, I tighten my arms around her. "You said you had a boyfriend in high school who was a Daddy. Tell me about him."

I don't really want to hear about this other man, but I want to know everything about my girl, so I'll keep my jealousy in check for the moment.

Cali lets out a soft sigh and relaxes into me. Even though I hate the guy, I get the feeling he was good to her, so I guess I'll let him live another day.

"He was the only boy at school who ever showed any interest in me. He was on the football team, but he wasn't like the rest of the jocks. He didn't go to parties or get into trouble. The first time we hung out, he was actually tutoring me in advanced algebra. I was so frustrated with myself because I always got good grades, but I couldn't grasp that subject no matter how hard I tried.

"He was so patient and helped me through it, then asked me on a date afterward. Neither of us had any money, so we went to a public park and he offered to push me on the swings. I couldn't remember a time I'd laughed so much or felt so free. He kept telling me to relax and enjoy the moment. I think I played on the entire structure that night, going down the slides, climbing on the monkey bars, going on the swings at least a dozen times. The entire time, he watched me and encouraged me and reminded me to be careful when I was climbing up stuff. It was the first time in my life I felt looked after.

"We started dating, and he took care of me. He'd make sure I had enough water or ate enough. He told me almost every day he wanted me to go to bed by nine. One night, we'd been talking on the phone for hours, and he called me Little girl and told me it was time for bed. I replied with 'yes, Daddy,' and he went totally silent. I thought I had upset him, but when he finally spoke, he told me he was thrilled I finally realized he was my Daddy.

"He explained how he'd learned about the lifestyle a couple of years before and knew right away he was meant to be a Daddy. I liked the way he took care of me and made me feel so innocent and carefree. Calling him Daddy aroused me. I think that night was the first time I'd ever touched myself and almost instantly had an orgasm. I knew right then that having a Daddy was what I wanted. I thought maybe he would be my Daddy forever, but then graduation rolled around and things were difficult at home. I was struggling to pay the bills because my mom was spending her money on alcohol, so I was stressed and not really able to give him the attention he wanted or needed, I think.

"He enlisted in the military. A week before he left for basic training, he broke up with me and told me he didn't want to keep me tied down while he was gone. I think it was more that he knew my life was chaotic, and he wanted someone who wasn't quite so messy to be with. He was good to me while we were together, and I understand his reasons for breaking up with me. He deserved better."

I close my eyes and silently thank the man who took care of my girl before I met her. I hate him for hurting her, but if he hadn't, I don't know if she'd be here with me now. "Have you seen him since?"

"He was married to someone else like six months later. I think they might have started talking before we broke up. I'm not sure. It didn't really matter. I don't think I was in love with him. I loved having a Daddy and experiencing the lifestyle, but we were very different."

"I'm so sorry, baby girl."

She rolls onto her back so she's looking up at me. "I'm not. He showed me who I was, and I'm always going to be thankful for that. I also know I wouldn't be here with you if it weren't for him breaking things off."

Neither of us say anything for several minutes, instead I stroke her cheek with my thumb and stare down into her beautiful eyes.

"I'm glad you had him in your life. He was an idiot for letting you go, though. Fucking moron."

Cali nods and smiles. "Me too. He showed me how a good Daddy should be. I wish Scarlet would have had the same experience. She so badly wants someone to love her that she doesn't pay attention to all the red flags."

"Don't worry, baby girl. Once we get her back, your Daddy will make sure any guy she considers dating is fully vetted and threatened within an inch of his life before he can date her."

That makes her giggle, and I love that sweet sound. Being the one to make her giggle is even sweeter.

"He'll know if he fucks up in any way he'll be getting fed to the fish," I add.

She laughs harder until tears are rolling down her cheeks. "I *knew* you fed people to the fishies!"

I burst out laughing and shake my head as I start tickling her until she's wiggling and trying to dodge my fingers.

"Wait! I'm gonna pee! Stop! Daddy! Mercy!"

As soon as I stop tickling her, she shuffles out of bed and runs to the bathroom, giggling the entire way there, and I'm pretty sure I have a perma-grin on my face. I don't remember ever smiling or laughing as much as I do around her, and it's an unfamiliar but welcome feeling.

When she emerges from the bathroom, still completely naked, she tiptoes back to the bed and crawls in next to me, positioning herself so her back is against my front. My cock is rock hard, and even though we will be married within a few days, it's going to be complete torture waiting to fuck her.

I nuzzle my face in her hair and wrap my arms and legs around her. "Goodnight, baby girl. Sweet dreams."

"Night, Daddy."

She's sleeping so peacefully when I wake up. The last thing I want to do is leave the bed, but I need to get to work. I have a list of things I need to do, including meeting with my men and getting a plan in place for war. My goal is to keep as many of my men alive as possible. Ivan and his men are about to find out what happens when you cross the wrong people.

I also need to schedule a meeting with Alessandro. Ivan told me he suspects the Italians, but I bet he's told Alessandro something different. There is no doubt in my mind that Ivan is the one responsible for his father's death. He might not have been the one to pull the trigger, but he definitely ordered it. While Vladimir might have been from a different syndicate, he was still a decent leader and held true to the pact that all of our families kept in place.

Slowly, I peel myself away from Cali and climb out of bed, then make my way into the guest room and grab Snickers to take the stuffed wolf back to my room with me. I slide the soft toy into her arms and smile when she sighs and burrows down into the blankets with the stuffie clutched to her chest. I can't even begin to describe how fucking happy it makes me that she got a stuffed wolf and named it Snickers after we met at Surrender. I wasn't the only one affected that night.

She's still asleep when I come out of the bathroom, showered and dressed in a black suit. I take one last look at her before I make my way down to the kitchen to get a cup of coffee to take to my office. Grace is already there making breakfast, but as soon as she sees me, she stops and smiles. "Good morning. I'll get your coffee."

I offer her a grateful smile and lean my hip against the counter. "You heard about us getting married?"

Grace smiles as she pours the dark, steaming liquid into a mug. "Yes. How exciting. Cali is such a sweetheart. She's the perfect Little girl for you. I have a feeling she'll run circles around you, but you need that."

"Yes. She is. I was wondering if you'd be willing to spend time with her while she tries on dresses. She's never really had a decent mother figure in her life, and with her sister being gone… I don't want her to have to pick out a dress all alone."

The older woman beams at me as she sets my coffee in front of me, and I notice her eyes look a bit shiny. Grace wasn't able to have children and has told me it was her greatest letdown in life, so I have a feeling doing this for me means more to her than I'd first realized.

"I would absolutely love to. I can help her with her hair too. If she wants, of course," Grace replies.

I nod and offer her a smile. "I'm sure she would love that. I'll have some dresses brought in this afternoon. If she doesn't find anything she absolutely loves, let me know and I'll have more brought in. And anything else she wants or needs."

"I know you will. You're a good man, Declan. A very good man. I know you think you're not, but you are."

Grace has been telling me this for as long as I can remember, and while I don't really believe her, it's still nice to hear. Even though she and I aren't related in any way, she's been here for me ever since my mom passed away when I was in my twenties. I'll be forever grateful for having her in my life — and in Cali's life.

"Thank you, Grace. Have a good day."

"Oh, I will!" she sing-songs back.

I'm smiling when I walk into my office. Killian is already sitting with a laptop in front of him and a scowl on his face. His clothes are rumpled and he has dark circles under his eyes along with a day-old beard.

"Have you been up all night?"

He glances up at me and nods. "Aye. I've been searching. I reached out to Hawk and asked if he and his brothers could help in searching for Scarlet's location."

I nod. Hawk Kingston and his seven brothers aren't part of our organization, but Killian and I consider them trusted friends. We help each other out when needed and right now we can use all the help we can get.

"You need to sleep. You're not going to be any use to me if you're dragging your arse all day."

Killian flips me off. "When have I ever dragged my ass? I'll sleep when Scarlet is found."

I raise an eyebrow as I lift my coffee mug to my lips, and I'm wondering why Killian is so deeply involved in this. He doesn't even know Scarlet. The only thing I can come up with is that he knows how important it is to me and Cali.

"Go shower and shave. We need to have a meeting with Alessandro."

Killian nods and leaves me alone. I spend the next hour making phone calls and getting things in place. Our wedding might not be anything big or extravagant like she deserves, but I'm going to make it as special for her as I can. While she may not have been treated like a priority as a child, she will always be my priority, and putting a smile on her face will always be my focus.

21

CALI

As soon as I shuffle out of Declan's room with my hair still a mess and only wearing one of his clean white T-shirts that goes down to my knees, I immediately run into Ronan in the hallway. I slow my steps, unsure of what to say. I haven't spent any time with him one on one, and quite frankly, he scares the shit out of me.

Not only is he tall, muscular, and tattooed like the rest of them, but he has a long scar on his left cheek that makes him look even more dangerous. Add on the constant scowl he's sporting, and it makes me consider tucking tail and running back into the bedroom. Declan assured me I could trust his men, so I stay where I am until he approaches me.

"Morning, lass. Get dressed. Your Daddy laid out clothes for you in the guest room. You and I will be spending time together today. Come down to the kitchen for breakfast when you're done."

My eyebrows pull together as I look up at him, trying to size him up and down. I want to sass him and tell him he's not the boss of me, but I'm pretty sure it would get back to Declan, and then I'd get my butt spanked. Or Ronan would just laugh in my face and threaten to take me with him over his shoulder like that big buffoon Grady had. I'm still a little salty toward that big butthead.

Ronan gives me a half lifted smile. "It's going to be fun, lass. I promise. Don't be a brat so early in the morning. I haven't had enough coffee for that yet."

Okay, maybe Ronan isn't so bad. Terrifying looking, yes, but he doesn't seem as scary as he looks. I let out a sigh and nod. "Fine. Where's Declan?"

He raises an eyebrow. "Your *Daddy* had to leave to meet with another syndicate leader. He'll be home by dinner, but he said he'll call you to check in around lunchtime."

I don't miss the way he emphasized the word Daddy. The reminder Declan gave me about calling him Daddy all the time comes to mind, and I realize he even wants me to call him that in front of his men. Of course, I know if I told him it was a hard limit, he wouldn't force it, but I don't think it is. It's just something I need to get used to.

I'm bummed I didn't get to see my Daddy before he left, but I have a feeling the meeting he's going to is all because he's trying to find my sister, so I can't complain. I'm grateful for him and all of his men being so willing to step up to help a stranger. It's also a good reminder to me not to give these guys such a hard time. While they all might be bossing me around constantly, they're just doing what my Daddy is telling them to do. They're following his orders, and I should be following theirs. So, I let out a sigh and nod. "Okay. I'll be down in twenty minutes."

Ronan nods, and without a word, turns around and heads toward the stairs. I'm left staring at his back for several seconds with a silly smirk on my face. He's definitely an interesting one. I'm not sure about him, but I also kind of like him. Although, now I'm wondering what he and I are going to be doing together today. He said it would be fun, but I have a feeling his version of fun and my version of fun are two totally different things.

When I walk into the guest room I had been staying in, I notice the clothes Declan laid out for me on the bed along with a note next to them.

Baby girl,

Killian and I have some business to take care of today. I'll try to be home by dinner. I expect you to eat your breakfast and lunch, and Ronan has been told to feed you himself if you don't. If he has to feed you, your bottom will pay the price when I get home. I have a fun day planned for you. Please be a good girl and don't give Ronan too much trouble. If you behave today, I'll give you a special reward tonight. Brush your teeth and put your hair up into pigtails today.

—Daddy

I let out a sigh and read the note several times. This man seriously knows how to make my knees weak. He also doesn't seem to understand the threat of a spanking doesn't really do much to detour me from being naughty. Although, pleasing him and getting a special reward has appeal too. Especially if that reward is his mouth on my pussy until I'm begging for mercy. The man has some sort of special tongue talent. It makes me wonder if he's as talented with his cock. I have a feeling he is.

The outfit he picked out for me is cute and surprisingly well matched. I'm not sure I'd be brave enough to choose something like this on my own, but I love it so much. The panties are a pair of cotton briefs that will surely come up past my belly button and have little wolves printed all over them. They make me smile as I slide them up my legs. The panties alone make me feel Little. The next piece of clothing is a pair of white capri-length leggings then a tutu to go over them that is so full and frilly I can hardly stop myself from squealing as I do a spin in front of the full length mirror. When I pick up the light pink T-shirt that matches the shade of the tutu, I realize there's no bra. Furrowing my eyebrows, I look around but don't see one anywhere. I don't have big boobs, but I never go without a bra during the day. After double-checking that there's no bra anywhere, I hesitate as I pull the T-shirt over my head and tuck it into the tutu. My nipples harden as they press against the fabric, and I wonder if Declan purposely kept me braless to make me feel more innocent. If that's the case, it's working. I'm beaming as I look at my reflection. I look and feel so young, and every so often, I do another spin so I can watch the tutu flare out.

There's a pair of white, brand-new slide-on Vans next to the bed, and I'm surprised when they fit perfectly. I probably shouldn't be. It's Declan. He's been stalking me for months. A little fact that should totally freak me out but it doesn't. It warms me from the inside out instead. He's been watching me, taking care of me, wanting me, all from a distance.

With a smile on my face, I go to the bathroom and find a hairbrush, two hair bands, and two pink ribbons sitting on the counter for me along with my toothbrush sitting out with toothpaste already on it.

He thinks of everything and always seems to be two steps ahead. The time he took this morning to pick out my outfit, set out my hair supplies, put toothpaste on my freaking toothbrush for me…it chokes me up, and I can't believe how lucky I am.

I spend the next few minutes brushing my teeth and then trying to get my hair into matching pigtails, but I can't get them right. With each try, I'm getting more and more upset. I'm two seconds away from stomping my foot when there's a knock at the bedroom door. I have only one pigtail up as I go to answer and find Ronan standing on the other side looking just as terrifying as he had a little bit ago.

"It's been forty-five minutes, lass."

My shoulders drop, and I feel bad for making him wait longer than I promised. "I'm sorry. I can't get my stupid pigtail right."

I hate that my voice is shaky and whiny when I speak, but I'm close to a meltdown which isn't something I'm used to. Ronan reaches out and takes hold of my wrist, making me startle, but then he leads me into the bathroom, leaving me standing facing the mirror. As though it's no big deal, he picks up the brush and silently works the other half of my hair into a pigtail then ties the ribbon around it. When he steps back and I look in the mirror, I'm shocked to find my hair is perfect and even. My eyes widen as I look back at him, but he just shrugs.

"Need to go potty before we go down?" he asks.

Oh, God. I want to die of embarrassment. Declan told me they were all Daddies, but I hadn't expected them to take care of me in his absence. Normally I'm a strong, independent woman but for some reason, dressed in these clothes, being surrounded by all of these alpha men, I feel so different. Like I can lean on them and trust they'll take control when I need them to.

I shake my head. "No. Thank you for fixing my hair."

Ronan winks and leads me out of the bathroom. "Do you need anything else before we go?"

"Where are we going?"

"Just to another part of the house. Come on. I think you'll like it."

I eye him suspiciously but follow him through the house, going through halls I haven't even seen yet or knew existed. The farther we go, the less homey it starts feeling. Is he leading me to a dungeon so he can chain me up and torture me? The very thought makes me giggle because even though we're walking in a weird area of the house, I know that's not what Ronan is taking me to do. These guys are scary but I feel safer around them than scared.

We come to a heavy metal door. He has to use his eye to scan us in, and then we're met with another big metal door right after that. He uses another eye scanner, and this time when we step through the threshold, we're in a giant room filled with guns and artillery and any type of weapon that could be imagined. Now I'm not so sure I should have trusted Ronan. Maybe he really is going to kill me.

His laugh causes my attention to snap up to his face.

"Relax, lass. We're here because I'm going to teach you to shoot a gun. You'll never be allowed to carry a gun on you, but being the wife of a mafia boss can be dangerous, and if there ever comes a time that shit goes down and you're on your own, I want you to be able to fire any gun you can get your hands on."

My eyes must be the size of saucers because Ronan looks fully amused as he smiles at me.

"Have you ever fired a gun?" he asks.

"No."

Even though guns scare me, I'm also a little excited. I've thought about getting a firearm many times over the years to protect myself in the city, but I've always been too afraid because I have no clue how to use one. I suspect Ronan is a pro at them, so maybe I'll feel a little better after he teaches me.

"I suspected so. Normally you would want to learn to fire a gun that fits your hand, but the likelihood of you grabbing a random gun that will fit your grip is slim, so we're going to start with one that fits, and then we'll practice on all different sizes and weights of firearms. Make sense?"

I nod, though I'm not really sure it does make sense. Why

would I be grabbing a random gun? And if I'm not going to carry my own gun, why do I even need to learn to shoot one?

"First lesson in mobsters. We always have more than one gun on us. There are three places we usually have one. Inside our boot, the back waistband of our pants, and one or two strapped to our chest." As he's telling me all of this, he's showing me all the guns he has on him and my mouth is hanging open. I would have never known there were guns under all their suits. I mean sure, I guess I knew they carried all the time, but I never truly thought about it.

Ronan leads me to a counter where there are dozens of firearms lined up, some so small they could fit in a tiny purse, and some so large I'm not sure how anyone could even use them. I'm disappointed when I see they're all black, but I guess gangsters don't want to carry around a pink gun.

"You need to assume every single one of these weapons is loaded and ready to fire. It doesn't matter if you know they aren't or if you know the safety is on. You always need to treat them as though they're loaded, which means when you pick one up, you keep it pointed toward the ground, and don't ever aim it at someone unless you're ready to shoot. Understood?"

I nod and watch as he picks one up from the counter, keeping the tip of it pointed down.

"Pick one up just like I did."

After scanning the variety of them, I reach for the smallest one and am surprised at the weight of it for how tiny it is. It's heavy. Cold, smooth metal against my fingers.

Ronan puts his firearm down, steps closer to me, and spends the next twenty minutes explaining all the parts of the particular gun I'm holding. Next, he takes it apart and explains how the inner mechanisms cause the weapon to fire. It's fascinating. After he does the same thing for three more of them, he picks one that is still all together and hands it to me. "Okay, lass. Time to shoot."

My eyes go wide, and though I'm pretty sure I could pass a test with flying colors about how to take a gun apart and put it back together, I haven't the slightest idea on how to shoot.

My expression makes Ronan chuckle. "Don't worry, lass. I'm going to teach you just like I taught you all of that. We'll take it one step at a time."

I nod and relax a little, offering him a smile. "Thank you...for this. I'm sure spending the day with me doing this isn't exactly what you'd like to be doing."

Ronan's eyes darken a little, and he leans a hip against the counter as he crosses his massive arms over his chest. He isn't wearing his suit jacket, but he's still in black slacks, a black button down shirt, and fancy black dress shoes. The sleeves of his shirt are rolled up, though, showing off his many tattoos, and damn, the man looks intimidating as heck.

"Spending the day with my future sister-in-law is exactly what I want to be doing. Teaching you some self-defense so you're safer is something I want to do. I asked Declan if I could teach you. He didn't order me to do it. Whether you realize it or not, lass, you're part of this family now, and we want you here. We want your sister here too."

I swallow heavily past the lump forming in my throat. All these gangsters have been so kind to me, treating me like I'm family, and I don't think they realize just how much I need that.

"Thank you," I say with a shaky voice. "I care about your brother. I've had a crush on him since the first time he came into O'Leary's. Even though he and I don't know each other very well yet, I feel something for him I've never felt before, and I trust him. I trust all of you. I just hope you guys don't think I'm using him or any of you to get my sister back."

My eyes are pointed toward the floor as I speak because the lump in my throat is still there, and if I look Ronan in the eye, I might burst into tears. The shadow of his body gets closer until I see his shoes just in front of me.

Suddenly, his hand is gently grabbing my chin and forcing me to look up into his dark-green eyes. "I've known you've liked my brother since the first time we came into O'Leary's after you started there. It was obvious to all of us. We also know you're a good girl, Cali, and I've never seen my brother have feelings for anyone the way he has feelings for you. I don't give a fuck if you are using my brother to get your sister back because I know Declan is going to do everything in his power to make you the happiest Little girl alive, and I have no doubt you will fall in love with him. I just hope you can handle all the constraints that come with this life. It's not easy on women, and my brother and I are a bit overprotective when it comes to Littles. So not only will you have to deal with all of Declan's rules, you'll have to deal with ours too. You won't get away with anything, Little one, so I hope you like sitting on a warm ass because I have a feeling you will be doing it often."

I can't help but smile. These men are so dang bossy and have egos the size of elephants. Despite all of that, I can't help but put my gun down on the counter and wrap my arms around Ronan's waist as a tear slips from my eye. "Thank you," I whisper.

He awkwardly pats my back before he actually wraps his arms around me and gives me a squeeze. When he releases me and takes a step back, he nods toward the shooting range. "Let's go, lass. Time to learn. This will be our sibling bonding time from now on. Eventually I expect you to be able to shoot as good as me."

Pulling my shoulders back so I'm standing taller, I grin at him. "Oh, I'll shoot better than you, big guy."

Ronan snorts and rolls his eyes. "In your dreams, brat, but that's the attitude I like to see."

22

DECLAN

"You know I'll have your back in whatever you have to do. I've never liked Vladimir, and I can't stand his prick of a son."

I smile at my longtime friend. "I won't call on your guys to help us unless it's absolutely needed. My goal is to get Scarlet free with as few deaths as possible."

Alessandro nods as he stares into his drink. "I can't fucking believe he tried to put it on us. That bastard told me he thought it was you guys who killed Vlad. I wonder what he told the other bosses."

"I haven't talked to anyone else yet. I wanted to talk to you first. We're in good standing with everyone—including the cartel—so I doubt they'd believe anything Ivan spews from his mouth. I want to warn them, though, so they can prepare their men. As soon as Cali and I marry, I'm going to spread the word of what's coming."

"She must be really something, eh?" Alessandro smirks at me with a knowing look, and I kind of want to punch him, but I know he means well.

"She's...everything I don't deserve, but I can't walk away."

He swirls the gold liquid in his glass for a long moment before he raises his gaze to mine. "We might not be good men, Declan, but that doesn't mean we don't deserve love. Everyone in the world has committed sins, some worse than others. We do what we have to do because we were born into it. This wasn't a choice we had. The person you fall in love with isn't a choice either."

My breathing goes shallow as I soak in his words. Alessandro and I are close in age, but he's always been more deep thinking than me.

"I don't want to corrupt her. She's so fucking pure and innocent and everything I'm not."

Alessandro smiles. "I know you'll do everything in your power to keep her shielded from this life. Besides, while you might corrupt her, she might soften you a little. It's a fair trade."

I smile at my friend and nod. "When the fuck did you get so damn deep?"

He laughs and shrugs. "We're getting old, my friend. Every year that passes without a sweet Little girl to come home to, the more I realize what's really important. It doesn't matter that I'm surrounded by men all day, every day. I'm fucking lonely, and it's the kind of lonely only someone special can fill. You might be a bad man to the outside world, but for her, you can be everything she needs, so don't hold back. You never know if you'll be here tomorrow."

Those words settle deep inside me. I might be a bad man, a monster even, but for her, I'll be anything she needs me to be for the rest of the life I'm given, and I'll make damn sure that once I'm gone, she'll be taken care of.

I lean forward and put my elbows on my knees, hating the next thing I'm about to ask. "I need a favor."

"Name it," Alessandro says.

"Ivan is going to know I'm coming after him, which

means my men, all of our real estate, and anything we touch will be at risk. I don't want Cali anywhere close to any of it."

Alessandro studies me for a long moment. "You want me to protect her since they won't suspect her being with the Italians."

I clench my jaw and nod. I fucking hate the idea of her not being near me, but if it means keeping her safe, I'll do whatever I need to do, and there isn't anyone else with the amount of security he has.

"I have a piece of property just outside of Seattle. It's gated with armed guards and heavy surveillance. She can go there, and I'll send a dozen men and some dogs to stay and watch over her."

"You're sure it's safe there?" I ask. It's probably insulting to ask such a question. Alessandro takes security just as seriously as I do, but when it comes to my Little girl, there's no such thing as being too careful.

"As secure as a maximum security prison. Just with better amenities," Alessandro says with a smile.

"Thank you."

He nods and reaches out to shake my hand. "I'll be at the wedding. Just tell me the date and time."

I shake his hand and rise from my chair. When I turn and leave, Killian follows me out of the room, and as soon as we're in the waiting SUV, he whistles.

"What?" I snap.

Killian chuckles. "Cali is going to have a fucking fit when she finds out you're sending her away to keep her safe."

I shrug. "She doesn't get a choice in the matter. Her safety is my responsibility, and if she wants to have a fit, she can have a fit, and then she'll be on her way to Alessandro's safehouse with a very red ass."

That makes Killian laugh harder and shake his head at the same time. "Good luck, boss."

Yeah. I have a feeling I'm going to need it.

I pull out my phone and check my messages to see what updates Ronan has sent me about my girl. There are half a dozen updates along with a photo he sent of her practicing in my shooting range. My first reaction when my brother had asked me if he could teach her how to shoot was to say fuck no, but the more I thought about it, though I hate the idea of her ever having to use a gun, I know in this life she may have to protect herself one day.

After reading the messages, I call her and wait three rings before she answers.

"Hi, Daddy!"

The soft sound of her voice and her calling me Daddy is enough to practically melt me. This woman has me by the fucking balls, and I don't even hate it.

"Hi, baby girl. How's your day going?"

"Good! Ronan taught me how to shoot. I'm better than he is now."

I chuckle because I have no doubt my girl is taunting my brother and telling him the same thing.

"I bet you are. I'm proud of you. How was lunch?"

"Oh, it was good! I had a sandwich and some watermelon and chips."

"Ronan said you only ate a quarter of your sandwich, refused to eat more than one bite of watermelon, and only had two chips."

The line is silent for several seconds, and I know my girl is trying to figure out how to get out of the little fib she just told me.

"Yeah, well, Ronan's a snitch, and snitches get stitches, Daddy. Or a finger cut off. I should cut off one of his fingers."

I can barely contain the laughter bubbling up in my chest. My girl is a spitfire, and I love her, but I'm a little worried about her infatuation with cutting fingers off.

"Cali Ann, I swear—"

"You shouldn't swear, Daddy. It's naughty. You told me not to swear. You said I might get soap in my mouth if I swear. Do you want soap in your mouth?"

Jesus Christ.

"Cali Ann Jenkins..."

She lets out a heavy sigh. "Okay. I'm sorry, Daddy." She sounds so fucking sad, it makes my heart ache. "It's just that I miss Scarlet so much, and it makes my tummy upset, and it's just, when you feed me it's easier for me to eat."

Now we're getting somewhere. My poor girl is hurting.

"I'm sorry, baby girl. I didn't realize that's why you weren't wanting to eat. I'll tell you what. I'll make sure I'm home by dinner so I can feed you, okay?"

"Okay," she replies quietly.

"Good girl. I have some wedding dresses being delivered in about an hour. Grace is going to help you try them on."

I hear her softly gasp. "You don't have to do that, Daddy. I can just wear one of my dresses I brought. It's not like it's a real wedding."

My jaw clenches so hard my back teeth ache and my palm itches to spank some sense into her.

"It is a real wedding, Cali. It's our wedding. It may not be the wedding you've always dreamed of, but it is as real as any other wedding. One day, I'll give you a big beautiful extravagant wedding that you deserve with your sister standing at your side, but for now, I'm going to do what I can to make this one as special as I can for you. So try on the dresses, pick any one you want, and if you don't find something you like, tell Killian and he'll have more brought in. Understood?"

It's quiet again, and I'm prepared to scold her if she argues with me again.

"Okay. Thank you," she whispers.

"You're welcome, baby. I'm thinking tonight after dinner,

we'll snuggle up in the living room and watch a movie. Sound good?"

"Really?"

I smile at the perkiness in her question. She likes the idea and so do I. "Yes, baby girl. It's a date."

23

CALI

"Cali, the dresses are here!" Grace sing-songs as she makes her way into the living room.

I smile because it's clear the older woman is just as excited about these dresses as I am. It's not a big fancy wedding, and honestly, I don't care about any of that, but knowing Declan had those dresses sent for me and that I get to pick any one I want means so much more than he could ever guess.

When Scarlet and I were kids, we would put on any piece of white clothing we could find and pretend we were getting married. We would have whole weddings in the living room of whatever shitty apartment we were living in at the time, and our ratty stuffed animals would be our guests.

The fact that my sister won't be here when I tie the knot with Declan saddens me so much I feel like vomiting, but at the same time, I'm doing this without her so I can get her back. I hope and pray she's okay. I'm trying my hardest not to think of all the horrible things they might be doing to her. No matter what she's going through, once she's home with me, I'll make sure she's okay. I know Declan will too. He may not love me, but it's obvious he cares about me, and I have a feeling he'll do just about anything to see me happy. Heck, the man is giving up his bachelor life just to help me. I owe him my life, and I vow to be the best wife I can be. I just hope he doesn't get bored with me and look for another woman to entertain him. Isn't that what mob bosses do? It seemed that that's what Ivan did to my sister. The thought of Declan with anyone else makes my heart break, and I realize it's because I'm in love with him that it hurts so much.

"Cali?"

I blink several times and smile at Grace who is looking at me with a worried expression.

"Sorry. Daydreaming. Where should I try on the dresses?"

The older woman's excitement returns, and she's practically beaming. It makes me wonder if she has kids of her own.

"I had them put in the powder room upstairs that's adjacent to the sitting room. I have champagne and charcuterie set up, too, so we can snack."

I'm touched that she went through all the trouble. The thought of food at all makes my stomach turn, but I don't want to disappoint her, so I smile and nod. "Sounds wonderful. Thank you, Grace!"

I grab my phone and follow her. As we make our way toward the stairs, Ronan comes from the opposite direction. I narrow my eyes at him, and as he passes us, I whisper, "Snitches get stitches."

He pauses mid-step and looks at me, fully amused, which just irks me.

"Excuse me, Little girl?"

I put my hands on my hips and tilt my head back to look up at the big ogre. "You're a tattletale. You told Declan I didn't eat my lunch."

His eyebrows rise, and he mimics me by placing his hands on his hips. I kind of want to kick him in the shins.

"My job is to report to your *Daddy* when he asks me to. Whether you like it or not, Little one, your health and safety come first, and if you're not being healthy or safe, I will tattle on you all day long."

I let out a huff and do the only thing I can think to do in the moment. I stick my tongue out at him. He stares down at me and starts laughing. The big jerk is laughing at *me*! How rude! He's definitely getting a finger cut off once I'm part of the mafia.

Grace giggles and grabs hold of my hand. "Come on, Cali, before you dig yourself into a deeper hole."

With a sigh, I make a face at Ronan before following Grace up the stairs to the large sitting room. Bash, Keiran, and Grady are all in there, making me freeze and look at Grace wide-eyed.

She smiles at me. "Every girl needs their girlfriends around when they're trying on dresses. These guys are the closest thing I could find. Now, go on. The dresses are in the powder room. Call out to me if you need help with any of them."

I hesitate and glance at the men who look less than enthused about being here, but Grace nudges me forward into the enormous powder room that could pretty much be a small bedroom.

When I close the door behind me and turn around, my breath catches in my throat as I take in all of the dresses hanging on a temporary rack. There are at least a dozen, all beautifully sewn, pure white, with lace and beads and crystals adorning each of them. They're absolutely stunning, and I have no doubt each one costs a small fortune. I can't bring myself to even touch them because I'm afraid of getting them dirty.

I sit on the closed toilet lid and open the messenger app on my phone.

> Cali: These dresses are so beautiful, but
> they're too expensive.

Almost immediately, three dots appear on the screen, and I wait nervously for Declan's response.

> Declan: They aren't as beautiful as you.
> Nothing is too expensive for you. I chose
> those dresses myself, and the cost is
> nothing to me. Pick one out, baby girl.

I nibble on my bottom lip, unsure how to respond. Part of me wants to obey, but part of me feels bad for the amount of money just one of those dresses will cost him. Three dots appear again.

> Declan: I'm not asking, Little girl. Pick out a
> dress, or you'll be going to bed with a red
> hot bottom tonight. You'll learn to obey
> Daddy one way or another.

His threat makes me smile. He likes to threaten me with a hot bottom a lot.

> Cali: So many threats. Sheesh. Do you
> threaten all your women with red bottoms?

My phone starts to ring with a video call almost immediately. As soon as I hit accept, Declan's stern face fills the screen, causing a shiver to run through me.

"Hi," I say nervously.

"I hope you're paying very close attention, Little girl. There are no other women. You. Are. It. I haven't entertained a single woman since the night I met you at Surrender, and I won't touch another woman for the rest of my life. You're mine and I'm yours. The only bottom I'll spank is yours, the only body I'll worship is yours, the only pussy, ass, and mouth I'll fuck and fill with my come is yours. You're the only woman I will kiss, tell my secrets to, share my feelings with, and share the rest of my life with. There will never be anyone else for me and there sure as fuck won't be another man in your life besides me. Tell me you understand that, Cali."

My eyes burn with tears, and all I can do is nod because my throat feels tight. No one has ever made me feel so wanted before. Not my father or my mother or my ex-boyfriend or anyone else. Declan makes me feel something I never even thought existed in real life, and it's raw and powerful in a way I can't even begin to explain.

"Say the words, Cali. I need to hear you say you understand everything I just said. Tell me you understand that you are mine and I am yours."

I nod again. "I...I understand," I choke out.

Approval spreads over his face as his eyes burn into me through the screen. "That's my good girl. Now, try on those dresses and choose one, otherwise I'm going to take my belt off tonight and spank your bottom until you understand that obeying me is in your best interest. Are we clear?"

"Yes," I whisper.

"Yes, *Daddy*. Don't think I don't know you've been calling me by my name in front of my guys."

That makes me smile. "Ronan is such a tattletale. I'm cutting off one of his fingers, Daddy. Maybe even two. He's a snitch."

Declan grins and rolls his eyes. "Just don't cut off his trigger finger. He's one of my best shooters."

I giggle and nod. "Fiiiiine, I won't. They always start with the pinkies first anyway."

He throws his head back and laughs, and I love the sound. He doesn't laugh a lot, so when I get to hear it—and especially when I'm the one to make it happen—it melts me into a pile of goo.

"You're my little savage. Now, go. Have fun and enjoy picking out your dress. I'll be home before dinner."

When the call ends, I look up at the dresses again, this time with a smile as I decide which one to try on first.

IT'S NEARLY six by the time Declan gets home. I'm sleepy because apparently trying on wedding dresses is more work than I thought. Grace seemed to have the time of her life as I was trying everything on while the men all nodded and smiled at each dress but didn't seem to have an opinion on any of them. Silly guys.

All of the dresses were beautiful and fit me perfectly, but when I put on the seventh dress, I knew it was the one, so I didn't try on any more after that. I hope Declan loves it as much as I do because as soon as Grace got all the buttons done, I felt like a beautiful princess. It's simple yet elegant, and the full skirt makes me feel like a Little girl playing dress up. Even though it's white, it reminds me of Belle's dress from *Beauty and the Beast* and I think that's why I love it so much.

"How's my baby girl?"

His voice makes my nipples bud into hard points, and my pussy clenches with need as he approaches me. Even though he's in a black suit as he always is, I swear he's more handsome today than he was yesterday. Maybe because it's the end of the day so he has a five o'clock shadow going on and his hair is a little tousled. He's drool worthy.

"I'm okay. Any news?" I ask hopefully.

His face is solemn as he shakes his head. "Not yet. But I'm working on a plan, and I have some friends outside of the mafia looking for her too."

I scrunch my face. "You have friends outside of the mafia? Is that even allowed?"

He chuckles as he wraps me up into his arms and pulls me to his chest where I automatically melt into him. "I'm the boss, of course it's allowed."

When I tilt my head back to look up at him, his eyes are already on me. It seems like they always are no matter who's around or where we're at.

"The marriage license will be ready tomorrow, so we'll get married tomorrow evening in the garden. After that, I'll try to get Ivan to give your sister up willingly, but if he won't, we'll do what we have to do to get her back."

"Okay," I whisper. "Do you have any idea where she even is?"

"No. My friend Colt is working on it. He's a tech guy so I'm sure he and his brothers are going over camera surveillance all over Seattle and Chicago to see if they can trace her steps. The last piece of information I got from Colt is that Ivan had texted your sister and asked her to meet him because he wanted to apologize and talk about things because he cares for her."

Anger boils within me. He tricked her, and my sister is so desperate for someone to love her that she fell for it. I rest my face on his chest, trying to keep my tears at bay, but I'm failing miserably. I want to kill Ivan myself and I've never wanted to truly hurt a person in my life.

Declan's warm hand touches my chin, and he hooks his finger under it so I'm forced to look up at him again. He leans down and kisses the tip of my nose with a light touch of his lips. "We'll get her back, baby."

I believe him. Declan might be a gangster, but there are a few things I already know about him. He's loyal, he's smart, and he's not the type of man to say something he doesn't mean.

"Thank you, Daddy."

He smiles softly and nods. "Let's go get you fed and then

it's movie night. I asked Grace to make something that would be easy on your tummy."

Before I can take a step toward the kitchen, Declan lifts me from the ground. "Wrap your legs around my waist."

I obey, and he carries me like a child with one arm under my bottom to support me on his hip. I snuggle right into him and rest my head on his shoulder, letting him take care of me because it's what I really need right now. I just hope one day I'm able to take care of him when he needs it.

Grace isn't in the kitchen when we get there, but the smell of herbs and spices makes my tummy growl. Of course, Declan doesn't miss the sound and narrows his eyes at me. "There will be no more skipping meals or only eating a tiny bit. I'll have my guys hand feed you if I'm not around to do it."

My eyes widen and I shake my head. "I promise to try to eat more. I can feed myself when you're not around."

He tilts his head. "Okay, but if I get any more reports of you not eating, they will be feeding you. Understood? My guys are not afraid to step in to take care of you if necessary."

"I understand, Daddy. I'll try harder."

"Okay. I just want you to be healthy, baby girl. Food and nourishment will keep you strong."

"'Kay, Daddy. I promise to try."

Declan sits at the table where the food is already set. But instead of sitting me in my own chair, he keeps me on his lap. There's a bowl of what looks like tomato soup and a grilled cheese sandwich cut into four pieces, and I lick my lips. Grilled cheese and tomato soup are my favorite, especially when I'm feeling down like I am now.

"What do you want a bite of first?" he asks.

I point to the sandwich, and he smiles and nods as he picks up one of the squares. For the next twenty minutes, he feeds me until I'm so full I'm practically groaning as I rub my stomach.

He chuckles and pushes the plates away before he nuzzles my neck. "Good girl. Thank you for eating. I guess you're too full for treats while we watch a movie, huh?"

I giggle and shake my head. "I'm never too full for treats."

He sets me on my feet, takes my hand, and leads me to the living room. I pause to take in the scene before me. Keiran, Bash, Grady, and Ronan are all seated on the couches. Keiran is holding two bottles of wine, Bash has a bowl full of Cheetos, Grady has a bowl of popcorn, and Ronan is holding two bags of sour gummy worms.

Declan smiles down at me. He reaches into his suit pocket and pulls out three king-size Snickers bars. "I know it's not the same as a movie night with Scarlet, but do you think it will do for now?"

Keiran goes to the wet bar and starts pouring the wine into glasses. When he brings one to me, I take the cup from him and grin. It's plastic and has Disney princesses all over it. He tugs on one of my pigtails. "I couldn't bring myself to buy cheap wine, but I promise you'll like it."

I smile up at him and take a drink. Holy crap. Expensive wine tastes so much better than the cheap crap I'm used to. "Thank you. This is yummy."

He winks at me and starts handing out glasses to the other men before taking a seat again. Declan leads me to the couch and takes my cup from me, setting it on an end table before he sits down and pulls me onto his lap. I turn and nuzzle into his chest, breathing in his scent, and I know I'm right where I'm supposed to be.

"Thank you, Daddy," I whisper.

"Anything for you, baby girl."

24

DECLAN

I always thought when the day came that I found a woman to marry that I would be nervous, but I can hardly wait to marry Cali. Even though I know she's already mine, the possessiveness inside of me wants it to be legal and have her last name be the same as mine. I'm fucked in the head and I know it, but I don't give a fuck. She seems to like me just the way I am.

Grace and Alessandro are our only guests other than my men. They will be the two people to sign our marriage license as witnesses. My men will stand on either side of Cali and me while the minister marries us. It's definitely not a traditional wedding, but I've done everything I can to make this day special for her.

My gardeners were here earlier to spruce up the grounds and make the garden pristine. The weather is warm and the sky is clear, so the sunset will be gorgeous as we're getting married. Grace has prepared a gourmet meal, and I had a wedding cake delivered this morning. The only thing missing is Cali's sister, and that makes my chest ache. There's nothing that can be done about it right now, but I'll make it up to my girl once her sister is back with us.

"Are you ready?" Killian asks.

"Never been more ready in my life," I reply.

The mood of the day isn't light and romantic like a wedding should be. We all know this is happening for a reason. It isn't unheard of for the mafia to have weddings that aren't filled with love. Some families marry out of duty, some to create alliances, and some to pay off debts. Even though this isn't any of those things, Cali doesn't know I love her yet, and I'm not sure how she feels about me, so the day feels heavier than it should.

I look at Killian and take a deep breath. "Thank you for being my best friend and having my back. I love you, brother. If anything ever happens to me, make sure she wants for nothing."

He smiles and gives me a back-slapping hug. "I love you too. Nothing's going to happen to you, boss. I'm happy for you. Seeing you two get married is worth getting punched in the jaw."

We step out of the small bedroom in the pool house where the six of us have been getting ready and go to the kitchen where Bash, Keiran, Grady, and Ronan are standing with shots of whiskey in front of them. I left the house to Cali and Grace to get ready this morning so I wouldn't see my girl until she's meeting me at the end of the aisle.

"We're waiting for you, brother. We need to make a toast," Grady says.

I walk over and pick up the waiting shot glass and listen as my brother makes a speech in Gaelic about loyalty, family, and love, but I mostly tune him out because the only thing I can think about is my baby girl. I hope she's not sad today. I hope she's looking forward to being my wife and my Little girl.

As soon as we down our shots, we make our way out to the garden where Alessandro and Grace are sitting in the only two chairs and the minister is waiting on us. Killian heads toward the house while the rest of us take our places and wait for the bride to be.

25

CALI

I look beautiful. My hair is pinned up into a fancy updo, my makeup is simple and perfectly applied, and the dress is the most beautiful piece of material I've ever worn. I'm excited and nervous all at the same time. If someone had told me two weeks ago I'd be getting married to a mafia boss, I would have laughed in their face. It's so interesting how things can change in the blink of an eye.

Hell, a week ago I was having nightly fantasies about the hot Irish customer who came in every week for lunch, dreaming about calling him Daddy and being his Little girl, and now I'm marrying that man and about to become his Little girl forever. If Scarlet were here, this day would be an absolute dream come true. Instead, it feels like a mix of a dream and a nightmare.

I hold a photo of me and Scarlet in my palm, and I can't stop the tears that have been threatening to fall for the past ten minutes.

"I miss you so much. I have so much to tell you. I love you. So much," I whisper.

The clearing of a throat startles me, and I look up to see Killian standing in the doorway of Declan's bedroom, a look of agony on his face. He gives me a small smile but I can tell it's forced.

"She knows you miss her, lass. I know she misses you too. We're going to save her."

Even though I haven't spent very much time with Killian, I can't stop myself from walking over to him and wrapping my arms around his waist. "Thank you."

He kisses the top of my head. "You're our family now so that makes her family. No one fucks with our family and lives to talk about it."

Those words should make me fearful of Declan, Killian, and the rest of the Irish mafia, but instead, they make me feel safe and loved. I've never had anyone fight for me or care so much about my well-being and happiness before.

"When we get our hands on Ivan, I'll let you at his fingers first. Deal?" Killian asks.

I giggle, thankful for him lightening the mood. I don't want to walk down the aisle and marry Declan while being sad.

"Can I cut off his dick instead?"

Killian winces. "Aye, lass. I didn't know you were such a savage. I don't think the boss would approve of you touching another man's dick, though."

We're both grinning and when Killian offers up his arm, I slide mine through. "Thank you, Killian. I know Declan is your best friend. I promise to be the best wife to him as I can."

He nods and swallows. "I know, lass. I see your love for him in your eyes."

I look up at him as we make our way down the stairs, and he winks at me.

"If you call him Declan again, though, I'm going to rat you out," he says quietly as we step out of the French doors that lead out the back of the house.

"Snitches get stitches," I murmur.

Killian laughs as we approach the garden, but the second I lay eyes on Declan, all of my humor disappears and I can barely breathe.

Declan is grinning at me, and as soon as I'm close enough, he reaches for me and takes me from Killian's hold.

The minister talks, but I barely hear any of it because I can't focus on anything other than my Daddy. When it comes to saying vows, we each repeat the words, and I'm thankful they are short and sweet because it feels like there's sand in my mouth. I'm nervous as hell, but it feels like a good nervous energy. Excitement bubbling, threatening to boil over.

"Do you have rings?" the minister asks.

"Yes," Declan replies.

I furrow my eyebrows because we hadn't talked about rings. It hadn't crossed my mind, and I feel bad because he got me a ring and I didn't get him anything. But then Killian hands something to Declan and then holds his hand out to me. He drops a solid black band into my palm and smiles at me before he steps back to take his place next to Declan again.

I'm in silent shock as Declan takes my left hand and slides a ring on my third finger. When I get a glimpse of it, I gasp. It's enormous. A light pink cushion-cut stone that is surely several carats big, sitting on a simple white gold setting. I look up at him, my eyes wide.

"I found the rarest pink diamond I could on short notice. The second I saw it, I knew it was perfect for you. You're a rare and beautiful diamond, Cali, and I want you to always know just how precious you are."

It's everything I can do not to throw my arms around his neck and sob into his chest, but I keep my composure long enough to slide the wide black band onto his tattooed ring finger. I never knew what a turn on it could be to slide a ring on a man's finger, but damn, my pussy aches with need as I do.

"With the power vested in me and the state of Washington, I now pronounce you husband and wife. Sir, you may kiss your bride," the minister says with a smile.

Before I can prepare myself, Declan crashes his mouth to mine and kisses me like we're the only two people around. One of his hands is threaded in the back of my hair while his other hand slides down to my bottom, squeezing it as he thrusts his tongue between my lips. I let out a soft moan into his mouth and kiss him back, my arms looped around his neck.

When I realize people are clapping and cheering, I smile against his mouth and he pulls back, grinning at me.

"Can we go fuck now?" I ask breathlessly, only loud enough for him to hear.

He throws his head back and laughs but then scoops me up and starts making his way toward the house.

"We'll be down for dinner in an hour. If we're not, eat without us," he calls out.

More clapping and cheering from everyone makes me blush, and I hide my face against his chest until we're alone in the house and he's making his way up the stairs.

He kicks the bedroom door shut behind us and sets me on my feet, his eyes trailing up and down my body.

"You look like the most beautiful princess in the world in that dress," he murmurs as he starts walking around me. "So fucking perfect. Daddy's princess."

A shiver runs through me as he presses a kiss to my shoulder blade before I feel his hands opening the back of my dress.

"As beautiful as you look, I need to see you naked and at my mercy."

I let out a soft moan as he presses another kiss to my other shoulder and then sinks his teeth into the crook of my neck. Declan isn't normally so gentle, and I know it's probably taking an incredible amount of strength for him to hold back. What he doesn't realize is, I don't want gentle. I'm not in love with him because he's gentle. I'm in love with him because of who he is.

"Daddy," I whisper.

"Hmm?"

He opens the last button of my dress, and it starts to slide down my body. I wiggle out of it until it's a pool of fabric on the floor around my feet and then turn around to look up at him.

"Please... I need you to be rough with me. Claim me, take me, make me yours like you did before. I trust you. I need you, and I need to feel everything."

His pupils dilate and his breathing turns shallow as he stares at my face. "Baby, it's going to hurt the first time I fuck you. I don't want to cause you pain."

The fact that this man doesn't want to hurt me means so much, but at the same time, I need the pain. I can't even explain to myself why I need it, but I do.

"Please, Daddy. Take control. Don't go easy on me. Make me yours. Take everything."

His tongue moves inside his cheek, and I can see his restraint dissolving, which only makes me more aroused. He's like a wild animal being let out of his cage, and he's going to do what wild animals do. Attack.

Before I can say anything else, his hand is wrapped around my throat, squeezing the sides. "What's your safe-word, Cali?"

"Red, Daddy."

I want this. I want his possession, and I need to feel like I belong. I want him to own me. Mind, body, and soul.

When he squeezes the sides of my throat tighter, I whimper and squirm under his hold, my nipples painfully erect and my panties completely soaked.

He steps closer so his face is nearly touching mine, and there's a look of pure, wild possession on his face. "You're going to be a good Little girl and do as Daddy says, aren't you, Cali? You're going to take my cock so good. So fucking deep inside your pussy, and I'm going to shoot my come deep inside you as your tight little cunt milks my cock."

The only thing I can do is nod, and cry out when he uses his free hand to pinch one of my nipples, twisting it just enough to cause a bit of pain that quickly morphs into pleasure.

My clit is throbbing, and I'm practically humping the air as he moves to the other nipple, keeping his eyes locked with mine the entire time. Everything in my mind is fuzzy, and I haven't even had a drop of alcohol.

"Daddy," I whimper as I reach for his suit jacket, pushing it off his shoulders.

He releases his hold on my throat just long enough to shrug out of his jacket while I work to unbutton his shirt before he pulls that off too. He's covered in tattoos all the way down to the waist of his slacks, and I love tracing the lines of them with my fingertips.

Without warning, he reaches down and rips my skimpy white lace panties from my body, dropping the pieces to the floor. He grabs my hips so roughly, I know I'll have bruises tomorrow, but that just makes my pussy ache more. I want his marks. I want to look in the mirror tomorrow and remember every single thing about this moment.

Declan takes a step toward me, pushing me until the backs of my thighs hit the bed, and he shoves me onto the mattress.

"Arms above your head. You move them, and I'm taking off my belt."

My arms fly up, making him chuckle. "Not ready to feel Daddy's belt on your naughty little ass? I have a feeling you're going to feel it often with as sassy as you are."

"I have to keep you grounded, Daddy."

He grins and grabs one of my ankles, rolling me onto my stomach before he starts peppering my bottom with his smacks. "Damn right you do, baby. And Daddy's going to keep you safe and protected and keep you from being a naughty Little girl. Ass up in the air, Cali."

I quickly move to raise my hips and as soon as I do, his fingers are in my folds, spreading my wetness to my clit.

"So fucking wet. Are you wet for me? Are you wet because you want Daddy's cock deep inside you?"

"Yes! Oh!"

With every flick of my clit, I can feel my orgasm building, and every so often when he spanks me, it spurs it on more until I'm moving my hips to meet his punishing hand. When he slides one finger inside me, I cry out and rock back against it.

"So needy, baby. Who knew you were going to be such a needy little thing?"

"Daddy! Please!"

"Please, what? What do you want, Cali? Tell Daddy."

My fingers are gripping the bedding so tightly, my knuckles are white, and I'm panting as I get closer and closer with each thrust of his finger. "Please, Daddy. Please make me come. Please!"

He chuckles and adds a second finger, curling them in a way that strokes the delicate spot inside me that makes me see stars.

"Come, baby. Come all over my hand. Take what you need, Cali. Fuck my hand, baby. That's it. Such a good fucking girl. Fuck."

I scream as my orgasm crashes through me while I continue to rock my hips against his hand, taking his fingers deeper and deeper with each thrust. I cry out over and over again, my pussy pulsing for what feels like several minutes, all the while he's continuing to finger fuck me until I collapse onto my stomach.

Declan chuckles and grabs my ankle, flipping me over again. "Sit up, baby girl. You're going to suck my cock before I fuck your perfect pussy."

It's a struggle to sit up because I feel like a pile of putty, but when he starts removing his pants and underwear, letting his cock spring free, I suddenly feel very energized as I reach for it. He steps forward, letting me wrap my fingers around the base as he guides it to my mouth. He's already leaking from the tip, and I can't resist licking it up before I open my lips and suck him in. As soon as I do, he groans and tilts his head back for a brief second before he looks down at me again.

"Good girl. Take it nice and deep, baby. That's a good girl. Fuck, you suck my cock so good. Do you know how much I love it that my cock is the only one you'll ever suck? It drives me fucking crazy, baby. You're mine. This mouth," he reaches out and cups my chin, "is mine to fuck for the rest of our lives. Your lips are so pretty wrapped around me."

I love his praise. It makes my pussy gush, and it turns me into a wild animal, sucking him hard and deep, gagging every time his cock hits the back of my throat.

"Fuck! Enough!" he growls, grabbing me by the hair and dragging me off his cock.

I whimper in protest but he ignores it. "You're going to fucking kill me, Little girl. Lie back and spread your legs. Show me what's mine."

I scramble into position. Every time he looks at my pussy, I know he loves what he sees. He doesn't hide his attraction, and he makes me feel like I'm the sexiest woman in the world. It only takes him a few seconds to roll on a condom, which is practically a hot porno by itself. Sheesh. Who knew that could be so hot to watch?

When he kneels between my legs, I suck in a deep breath

as his cock nudges the opening of my pussy. His forearms are resting on either side of my head, and he's staring down at my face with hunger in his eyes.

"It's going to hurt, baby."

"It's okay. Please, Daddy. I want you to take me. Don't hold back."

His eyes close for a long moment, and when he opens them, they're burning with desire as he nudges his cock into me. I squirm almost instantly as he stretches me and cry out from the pain. I knew it would hurt, I just didn't realize how much and that it would burn. He continues to inch in, and I continue to squirm, trying to adjust to his size.

"I'm so sorry, baby girl," he murmurs.

"Fuck me, Daddy. Please. Just get this part over with," I whimper, trying to grab his ass and pull him in deeper.

"Hold on, baby," he growls as he slams the rest of the way into me.

I scream and suck in a breath, unable to take another as the burning pain sears through me. Declan freezes, regret etched all over his face before he lowers his mouth to my neck and presses several soft kisses to my throat.

"Breathe, baby girl. Breathe for Daddy."

His words bring me out of the shock I'm in, and I do as he says, taking one breath after another until the pain starts to subside and slowly morphs into a feeling of fullness.

"Please move," I plead.

While keeping his eyes locked on mine, he slowly pulls out a little bit and then pushes back in several times until my pussy relaxes and adjusts to his size, the pain I'd felt just seconds before becoming pleasure.

"Oh. Ohhh."

He grins and winks at me as he starts picking up the pace. My hands roam his chest, and I run my fingernails down his pecs as he lowers his mouth to my breasts, licking and sucking my nipples one after the other until I'm panting and on the verge of orgasm again.

"I can feel your pussy tightening, baby. You're going to fucking kill me," he grounds out as he pumps into me.

Sweat coats our bodies, and we pant while I claw at his chest and his hands are gripping fistfuls of my hair.

"Come for Daddy. Come on my cock, baby girl. Milk me, baby."

That's all it takes for my body to obey and my second orgasm to explode. At the same time, Declan's thrusts become harder and more erratic until his entire body tenses and he lets out several low grunts as he pumps into me.

A slow smile spreads across my face, and I let out a deep sigh of contentment.

Declan is staring at me with concern. "Are you okay, baby girl?"

I nod. "Fantastic, Daddy. When can we do that again?"

His deep laugh warms me from the inside out, and I don't think I'll ever get tired of that sound.

"You need some time to heal. You're going to be sore, baby. Let's take a bath, and then we'll go have dinner and cake."

26

DECLAN

I've had a lot of sex in my life. Vanilla *and* kinky but none of those times even came close to how it felt with Cali. I hated hurting her, but fuck, being inside of her makes me feel like I'm home, right where I'm supposed to be. I hate that her sister was kidnapped, but damn, I feel so fucking thankful Cali came to me to help her.

As we sit in the tub of steaming water with her between my thighs, we're both silent for a long time, and it doesn't feel awkward or weird. We're completely content being in each other's arms.

"What happens now?" she finally asks.

I hate that our wedding day is overshadowed by her sister missing. The day is still special to me, but there's that dark cloud hanging over us.

"Now, we ask Ivan to release your sister willingly since she is legally part of the Irish mafia now. If he refuses, we go in forcefully."

"Do...do you think he's going to kill her?" she asks, her voice breaking.

"No. I think he's going to try to negotiate. He's a snake

and he wants power. He's going to try to negotiate her freedom for some of our territory."

She turns her head to look up at me, her eyebrows pulled together. "Are you going to do that?"

"Not a fucking chance in hell. But we'll make him believe we will while we work out our plan of attack. Ivan is an idiot. He's the type of guy who thinks he's smart, but he acts on impulse instead of logic. I've been in this business for long enough to know that impulse will get you killed. I have a feeling the men in his ranks aren't all happy he's the new boss. Vladimir was loyal to his men, and they were loyal to him. Ivan will use them and give no loyalty in return. In the mafia, loyalty is everything, so his men will only follow for so long before they go against him."

"Is there anything I can do to help?" she asks.

I tighten my hold around her and kiss the top of her head. "Just obey me and trust me. You might not like everything that has to happen, but it has to happen for a reason."

My words cause her to turn around and face me. "What do you mean?"

"Baby girl, if we go to war, I can't have you anywhere in Irish territory. Ivan will come after us, and he'll come after my weak spot, which is you. That can't happen. I won't allow it to happen."

Her face falls and I hate it. I'm supposed to be the one who makes her smile.

"So where will I go?"

"I have an alliance with the Italian mafia. Alessandro, he's the guy that came to the wedding, he's the boss and we grew up together. We're friends and we trust each other with our lives and have always helped each other out when needed. He has a property just outside of Seattle that isn't in my territory. If we go to war, you'll go there where you'll be safe with his army of guards."

Her eyes widen and her mouth drops open as she starts

to shake her head. "No! No. I'm not going to go anywhere without you."

"Cali, this isn't up for debate. I'm not risking your safety. It's the only option. I need my men to be available to go against Ivan, and the only organization he's going to go after is the one attacking him. You'll be safe with Alessandro. Who makes the rules in this relationship?"

When her bottom lip trembles, I feel my chest tighten.

"You do," she whimpers softly.

I pull her against my chest so she's straddling my legs and begin stroking her head. "I don't want to be away from you either. I fucking hate the idea of it, but you're precious to me, and I will not ever risk your safety. I love you, Cali. I know it's fast, and I know you married me for reasons other than love, but I do love you, baby girl. I have to take every precaution I can."

She sniffs and lifts her head to look at me. Tears are falling down her cheeks, so I reach up and wipe them away with my thumbs.

"I love you, too. I've never felt so safe and cared for until you, and at first, I wanted to marry you to get my sister back, but now it's more than that. I want her back more than anything, but even if she were here, I'd still want to be your wife and your Little girl."

I pull her back to my chest and tighten my hold on her, fighting the lump forming in my throat. I never thought anyone would be able to love me. I'm a monster, but even monsters need someone to soothe them. Cali is that person, and she loves me even though she knows what I am.

"Please, baby, please do what I need you to do so I know you're safe and I can focus on getting your sister back."

Because of the tight hold I have on her, she's barely able to move her head as she nods. "Okay, Daddy. Whatever you need me to do, I'll do it."

"Thank you," I whisper.

She sighs and pulls back to look at me. "But if Alessandro or any of his men are jerks, I'm cutting their fingers off."

I throw my head back and laugh. My girl. She's wild and sassy and definitely a handful, but she's all fucking mine.

By the time we've drained the bathtub, I've dressed Cali in a soft white cotton baby-doll dress I bought just for tonight, and we've made our way downstairs, everyone is already in the middle of dinner. As soon as we walk in holding hands, the room goes silent as they watch us take our seats. Cali looks to me, a blush on her cheeks, but I wink at her and start filling her plate with food. Instead of setting it in front of her, I set it in front of me and then snag her out of her chair and put her on my lap.

Her eyes widen and she tries to wiggle off my lap, but I give her a stern look and a shake of my head, which is all that's needed to make her sit still. I love that she can be so obedient sometimes and so sassy other times.

Everyone goes back to eating, and I start feeding my girl, taking bites of food for myself in between. The moan that escapes her lips when I give her a bite of the roasted chicken makes my cock jump in my slacks. I know she feels it because her eyes whip to mine as she pulls her bottom lip between her teeth.

"Easy, baby girl," I whisper as I hold a forkful of food up to her mouth.

Even though she gives me a pouty look, she opens her lips and eats her dinner like a good girl.

The conversation flows throughout dinner. Grace passes out cake and coffee then comes and gives Cali and me a hug before she goes home for the night.

Cali stands and wraps her arms around the older woman. "Thank you so much for all your help."

I can see tears shining in Grace's eyes, but she blinks

them away before they fall as she gives Cali a tight squeeze back.

When we're done with our cake, I nod toward Alessandro and rise, lifting Cali in my arms and settling her on my hip. I make my way through the house toward my office. Killian and Alessandro follow.

"Baby girl, I want to introduce you to Alessandro De Luca. He leads the Italian syndicate and is a close friend."

Cali looks up at him shyly but reaches out and shakes his offered hand.

"It's nice to meet you, Cali. You looked beautiful today. I'm happy Declan found such a wonderful Little girl to spend his life with."

Her eyes widen as she looks to me, clearly surprised by Alessandro's knowledge of her being Little. I pull her back toward me, wrapping my arms around her front. "Alessandro is a Daddy too. You're safe to be you around him."

She nods and smiles but doesn't say anything more, and I'm glad Alessandro seems to understand when I shift the conversation.

"I spoke with the Albanians and the Cartel. Ivan is blaming me for the death of his father. Of course, they don't believe a word the little fucker spews. I've warned the other syndicates of a possible impending war."

Alessandro nods. "You know we're all behind you in this just as you would be for us if it came down to family. I have a feeling there is some unrest going on with the Russians. By the time this is over, everyone but Ivan will probably be behind you."

We talk for a few more minutes before Killian walks Alessandro out, leaving Cali and me alone in my office. She turns toward me, looking into my eyes so I lean down and press a kiss to her soft lips, resting my hands on either side of her neck as my thumbs stroke her pulse points. When I pull back, she sighs. "Are you sure we can't fuck again?"

I chuckle and shake my head. "Such naughty words coming from such sweet lips."

"I learn from the best," she says with a giggle.

"Uh-huh. You're a naughty Little girl. You need your ass spanked soundly."

Her pupils dilate as she nibbles on her bottom lip. "You make a lot of threats, Daddy, but not a lot of action."

Oh, my sassy girl. She has no idea the bear she's poking. "You have five seconds to get upstairs, get naked, and get on the bed with your ass in the air. Otherwise, you're getting a plug in your bottom before I spank you. One."

Cali lets out a squeal and takes off running, giggling the entire way. I give her a small head start before I catch her at the top of the landing and throw her over my shoulder as I make my way into our bedroom. I won't fuck her while she's sore but that doesn't mean I won't plug her ass, spank her, and then feast on her pussy all night long. It is our wedding night after all, and quite frankly, I'm completely fucking addicted to this Little girl.

27

CALI

Declan gets me naked and bent over the edge of the bed so quickly I don't even know how he manages it. One of his large hands presses down on my back, holding me in place as he stands at my side, lecturing me.

"You're going to learn that being sassy and saying naughty words will get you put into this position often. Not that it's a hardship for me because Daddy loves looking at your ass."

I try to squirm, but it gets me a smack to my bottom, and I yelp.

"Stay right where you are, Cali. You move and I'll edge you all night without letting you come."

Well, that's just mean. Sheesh. Maybe I should threaten to edge *him* all night. The thought makes me smile. I don't think it would work out very well for my bottom if I tried that.

Like the good girl I am, I stay in place as he steps away from me. When he returns to my side, he drops something on the bed. I look down near my hip and see what I'm pretty sure is a butt plug, but before I can rise and protest, his hand returns to my back, pinning me firmly in place.

My pussy is soaked, and I know he can see it. He uses his free hand to slide his fingers over my lips, starting at my clit and moving toward my ass, spreading my arousal along with them. When he circles my tight ring, I whimper and shift my legs, unsure how I feel about the sensation. In one way it feels so naughty and taboo, but in another, I feel so damn submissive and turned on that he's doing whatever he wants with my body and I can do nothing about it.

That's not totally true. I know if I say my safeword, he'll stop, but I don't want to say it. I want to feel every sensation he's going to give me.

"Naughty Little girls get their asses stretched and plugged."

The tip of his finger breaches my asshole just slightly, making me whimper and moan before he pulls it away and I hear the cap of a bottle pop open. Cold liquid drips down my crack.

He returns his fingers to my bottom and slowly starts working one into me. The slight burn makes me squirm and try to move away from him but he doesn't allow me to get away. Instead, he holds me more firmly against the mattress as he presses in deeper.

"Daddy," I cry out breathlessly.

The mix of sensations is making my brain jumbled. It burns slightly, but it also feels good, and I feel so incredibly naughty but turned on at the same time.

"I know, baby. Take some deep breaths. Let Daddy in. That's a good girl."

He adds a second finger, and the burning becomes stronger but quickly morphs into something more pleasurable as he works them in and out of me. An orgasm is so close to the surface, and soon I'm wiggling my hips to meet his thrusts.

Just as I'm about to explode, he pulls his fingers free, making me cry out in protest. He chuckles, and I feel the cold tip of what I assume is the butt plug pressing into me.

"Take a deep breath in, baby, then let it out."

As I obey his instructions, he starts to press the plug into me, stretching me wider than his fingers before it pops into place, and I relax a little, panting against the bedding.

"Good girl. Maybe next time you decide to use dirty words or sass Daddy, you'll think twice?"

Before I can answer, he starts swatting my bottom, alternating cheeks.

"Ouchie! I'll be good!"

He chuckles in response and continues to spank me hard and fast, peppering my entire bottom. It isn't super painful, and I'm getting more and more turned on with each swat.

"Daddy!"

"Yes, baby girl? What is it?"

When he pauses just briefly and spins the plug inside me, I moan and squeeze my eyes shut. My clit throbs for his touch.

"Please! Please, I'll be so good. I'll be the goodest girl ever. I promise. Please just make me feel good."

I'd get on my knees right now and beg him for an orgasm, but apparently my plea is enough because suddenly he's the one on his knees behind me, spreading my lips and sucking on my clit until I'm screaming out an orgasm and trembling uncontrollably against the mattress.

I've given myself orgasms. Many, many orgasms over the years. Not a single one of them has ever felt like this.

The world is spinning around me, but I'm just a limp pile of goo, barely able to keep my legs from giving out. It's pure bliss. That's the only way I can describe it.

A moment later, I feel the plug being gently tugged from my bottom before Declan carefully lifts me onto the bed. I know I need to repay the favor, I just need a minute—or five

—to get my bearings. Surely his cock will still be hard in ten or fifteen minutes. Maybe twenty so I can sneak a short nap in because as each second passes, I float further down the path to sweet dreamland.

Something warm and wet against my pussy makes my eyes open, and I watch through slitted lids as Declan uses a cloth to wipe my pussy and ass clean with a look of adoration on his face. As soon as he's done, he gets rid of the towel and strips down to his boxer briefs before he climbs into bed, pulling me up against his body.

"Give me a few minutes," I murmur.

He chuckles. "A few minutes for what, Little one?"

"To suck your cock."

His hand strokes my hair, and his lips press to the back of my head. "Not tonight, baby. It's time for you to sleep. Daddy has you. Just rest."

His reassuring words and soft touch are all I need to allow myself to drift off to sleep.

I'M disappointed when I wake and Declan isn't in bed with me, but as soon as I open my eyes, a smile spreads because he's sitting in one of the arm chairs with a cup of coffee in one hand while scrolling on his phone with the other.

"Daddy."

His attention immediately shifts to me, and he gives me one of his breathtaking smiles I don't think I'll ever grow immune to.

"Good morning, baby. You seemed to sleep well."

Yeah. You could say that. I don't think I even moved all night. Who knew a few orgasms could tire a girl out so much?

He moves over to my side of the bed and sets his coffee on the nightstand before sitting down next to me. He's already fully dressed in a suit, and his hair is still damp from his shower, and damn, he looks edible. When he brings his hand to my cheek, I lean into his touch and sigh. As much as I love these little moments we have, I hate that they're clouded with my sister's kidnapping. My heart squeezes in my chest at the thought of her, wondering where she is and if she's okay. I don't think I'd be able to bear it if something happened to her.

"I want you to stay in bed and rest. I need to go down and get to work. I'll bring up breakfast in a bit and feed you."

"Will you keep me updated?"

"Of course. But I want you to rest. I'm sure you're sore today?"

Not wanting to lie to him, I give a slight nod. My entire body feels like I did a triathlon, and my pussy feels even worse. Not that I would change anything that happened last night, but yeah, I'm a bit uncomfortable.

He disappears into the enormous walk-in closet for a moment before he comes back with several flat boxes in his hands. "I got something for you."

I scrunch my face as I sit up, resting my back against the headboard. He perches on the edge of the bed beside me and hands me the boxes. My eyes widen as I stare at them, and I'm completely speechless.

"You got me bracelet making kits?" I finally ask.

"You told me the night we met it was something your Little liked to do. I thought it would be something you could do in bed if you got bored."

My sinuses burn with tears, and I sniffle, trying to keep myself from turning into an emotional mess. I can't meet his eyes because if I do, I'll start crying. I haven't made bracelets in so long. It's one of my favorite things to do, even if they are just silly, cheap little things.

"Thank you, Daddy," I whisper.

He leans over and kisses my forehead. "Anything for you, baby. Just promise me you'll make me one of your fabulous bracelets, okay?"

This makes me giggle because the idea of my mafia boss husband wearing a plastic piece of jewelry along with his Rolex is absurd, but I nod anyway. "Okay."

"I'll be back in a bit, baby. Call me if you need anything."

"I will."

He's almost to the door when he pauses and turns. "Cali?"

I finally look up at him and smile. "Yeah?"

"I love you, baby girl. You're special and precious, and I always want you to know that."

All I can do is nod as tears cloud my eyes. He gives me his breathtaking smile and disappears from the room, and somehow, I know everything is going to be okay, one way or another.

28

DECLAN

K illian and Bash are already in my office when I walk in. Killian has his phone in his hand with a call on speaker.

"Colt is on the line. He has something," Bash says.

I beeline for the seat next to Killian. "Hey, Colt. What do you have?"

"I've located her. I was able to track all her movements on camera from the time she left her apartment to where she is now," Colt tells us.

"Where is she?" I ask.

"She's at Vladimir Petrov's estate right here in Seattle. In one of the outbuildings. It's basically a concrete box with no windows and only one door."

Killian lets out a string of curses while I try to form my thoughts and figure out what to do next.

"Where is Ivan?" Bash asks.

Colt sighs heavily through the phone. "He's staying in the mansion. I was able to hack into their surveillance system and get access to all of their cameras. Ivan shot and killed his dad execution style the night of your meeting when they arrived back at the estate. He did it right out in the driveway in front of several of their men."

Fuck. This kid is such a fucking waste of space on this earth. I can't wait to kill him with my bare hands while he's looking straight into my eyes, because only a bitch shoots someone behind their back.

"Can you send me the footage of that?" I ask.

"It's already been encrypted and sent securely," Colt replies without a beat.

"Has anyone been going in or out of the building she's in?" Killian asks through a clenched jaw.

This time Colt hesitates to answer. "I haven't seen anyone go in or out of there since they locked her inside."

Killian shoots up from his seat, goes to the nearest wall and shoves his fist through it. Not that I blame him because the same rage burns inside me right now too.

"Colt, can you help us get into the property if we need to?" I ask.

I hear typing over the phone for several seconds before Colt replies, "I should be able to. The security system is a little tighter than the surveillance system, but give me some time and I'll be able to get in there."

We end the call with Colt, and I look to Killian and Bash. Killian is pacing the room while Bash is tapping the screen on his phone. A moment later, Keiran, Ronan, and Grady walk in.

"We need to call Ivan and ask him to voluntarily release Scarlet, but in the meantime, I want the video footage of him killing his father sent out to all the other heads so they know without a doubt who did it," I say.

Grady nods, moves behind my desk, and opens my laptop, getting to work on the video footage while I find Ivan's phone number in my contacts.

It only rings twice before Ivan answers. "Declan."

I'm barely able to hold in my sneer. "Ivan."

"What can I do for you?"

"You can release my sister-in-law immediately. Cali and I have married, making Scarlet part of the Irish family."

Ivan chuckles. "Kind of convenient you're suddenly married to Scarlet's sister just two days after you confirmed you weren't."

"Yeah, well, your refusal to release her moved up the wedding date," I say calmly.

My heart is thumping in my chest, and my pulse is racing, but I won't let this little punk know it. He's the type of fucker who would love to see me get angry and lose control. I won't give him the satisfaction. Instead, I'm going to keep my cool and piss him off.

"You need to release her immediately, Ivan," I add.

I hear him speak Russian to someone in the background before he speaks to me again.

"I'm willing to let Scarlet go. She's really worthless to me. Dumb bitch didn't fucking know how to satisfy me anyway, and she surely wouldn't make me any money if I put her out on the streets."

Killian looks as though he's going to explode, but I hold my hand up to stop him from saying anything.

"I'm willing to overlook her being taken if you release her now as long as she is unharmed," I tell him.

"You're willing to overlook it," Ivan scoffs. "I'm not willing to overlook the amount of territory you have, though. You want Scarlet back, you give me thirty percent of your territory in Seattle."

I knew it. I fucking knew he would try to negotiate.

"The territory we have is ours and has been for nearly sixty years," I say matter-of-factly. "We've taken care of our territory and the people in it."

"Yeah, well, things change, don't they, Gilroy? You want Scarlet, you'll give me what I want," Ivan snaps back.

"Has she been harmed?" I ask.

It takes him a moment before he replies, "No. The bitch hasn't been harmed. She's just been in a good long timeout to teach her a lesson."

I flex my fists, wanting nothing more than to drive them through this little punk's face as soon as I see him.

"What's it going to be?" Ivan asks.

He's speaking quickly, as though he's hyped up on something, and I wonder if he's been testing his father's product a little too much. This could be a good thing or a bad thing. Good if he isn't in his right mind to comprehend what's going on, but bad if he's not making sane decisions.

"Twenty percent of my territory, and I want her back within twelve hours."

I normally wouldn't give him that much time but I'm doing it for two reasons. First, I don't want him to know that *I* know she's in Seattle and second, if he thinks he has twelve hours, that gives me time to get Cali out of here and get my army of men ready to battle with the Russians.

"Are you stupid, Declan? This isn't a negotiation. This is a demand. Thirty percent or I slit her fucking throat," Ivan spews.

Yeah, he's right about one thing. This isn't a negotiation. I'm just trying to make it look like one so he thinks I'm actually considering it. He'll find out soon enough that I don't negotiate when it comes to my family.

I let out a deep, purposeful sigh. "Fine. Thirty percent. I'll get the documentation over to you, but you need to get her back to Seattle immediately, untouched."

Ivan sniffs loudly, and I hear him spit. I cringe at the sound. What Scarlet ever saw in this little fucker, I'll never understand, but I'll make damn sure she doesn't make the same mistake twice.

"I'll get her on a plane as soon as I see the paperwork."

The call ends and all of us let out a curse.

"Get Alessandro on the phone and have him send his men to get Cali. Grady, create some false documentation. Keiran, get everyone ready."

They all get to work as I leave my office and go to the kitchen to collect Cali's breakfast.

Grace is standing at the sink washing dishes when I walk in. She smiles at me but her smile drops when she sees my face.

"What's going on, Declan?" she asks as she wipes her hands on her apron.

"I need to send you to a safehouse, Grace."

She shakes her head. "I'm not going anywhere."

"Grace..." God bless this stubborn-ass woman but damn, why can't she make this easy on me?

"No, Declan. This is my home. I've lived on this estate for the past forty years, and you and everyone in this house are my family. I'm not leaving."

I let out an irritated sigh and narrow my eyes at her. "Don't make me fire you, Grace."

The older woman just laughs. "I'd like to see you try. Your mother would slap you from the grave if you did."

My mother was fond of Grace. They were great friends over the years, and my mother never treated Grace like she was different just because she was part of the help. Grace became my mother's confidante whenever she needed another woman to talk to, and my mother was there when Grace's husband, who was in my father's ranks, died. This woman is truly part of my family.

"Fine. You're staying in the mansion though. Go to your house and get whatever you need so you don't have to leave here, and if anything goes down, you get your ass to the saferoom."

She gives me a triumphant smile. "Such a foul-mouthed man."

"I love you, Grace. I don't want anything to happen to you."

"I know, Declan. I love you too. I'll be fine. I've been in this life a long time. I'll follow your overbearing rules to a T."

I sigh and nod. "Have Grady go with you to your house. He can carry whatever you need."

Grace has a cottage on the other side of my property, so she has privacy but is always close by if we need her. At least now, I know she'll be in my house that's guarded by dozens of men.

"I have to go tell Cali what's going on," I say as I grab the tray of food that's somehow still hot and steaming. I have a feeling Grace has been rewarming it every few minutes. It's one of the many reasons I'm so fond of her.

As soon as I step into the bedroom, my eyes find my girl, sitting up in bed with a tray of beads in her lap as she carefully strings together a bracelet. I smile at the sight, her tongue sticking slightly out of her mouth as she concentrates. Her hair is still messy from sleep, and I see she found one of my T-shirts to put on, which makes my cock stir in my pants. Seeing my clothes on her makes me even more possessive of her.

"Hey, baby."

She looks up and smiles as I make my way to her and set her breakfast on the nightstand. Her smile fades just like Grace's had when she scans my face.

"What's wrong, Daddy?"

I sigh and sit on the edge of the bed, facing her. "He won't give her up unless I give him some of our territory."

Her bottom lip trembles, and she drops the bead and string before setting it aside. "What now?"

"Now, we go to war. Alessandro and his men will be coming to get you soon."

A tear slips down her cheek, and I swear it makes my heart crack right down the middle. I hate seeing her upset.

"We did confirm she is alive and unharmed," I add.

Cali lets out a sob. "Are you sure? She's okay?"

I nod. "I don't know what kind of shape she'll be in, but he said she is unharmed. She's being held on his father's estate in what looks like some sort of concrete cell."

Her tears start falling, wetting her face, and she quickly tries to wipe them away as she nods. "I'm scared."

"I know, baby. It will be over soon. I need you to be a good girl for me and go with Alessandro. I need to focus on getting Scarlet back without worrying about you."

"Promise you'll come back for me?" she asks, her voice cracking.

I reach out and grip her chin, forcing her to look into my eyes. "I will always come back for you, Cali. You're mine. I will never let you go."

"Okay," she whispers.

IT'S FUCKING torture watching Alessandro's three SUVs drive away with my girl buckled into the middle car. I hate that I have to send her away, but my plan is to get this over as quickly as possible so I can bring her home and start our life together.

"We have snipers setting up outside of Petrov's estate and helicopters in the air a short distance away. The other syndicates have been notified and are currently on lockdown but prepared in case Ivan comes after any of them," Killian tells me as we get into our waiting SUV.

I have hundreds of men in my ranks who are armed and ready to storm the Petrov estate. Colt was able to provide us with basic plans of the property after sending his drones to capture camera footage, and he's already hacked into the security system, which will make it impossible for the Russians to electronically lock down the compound.

"Are you ready?" Killian asks.

Even though I have a strange feeling in the pit of my stomach that something is going to happen, I push it aside and nod. "Let's go."

29

CALI

I want to cry. Not just tears trickling down crying. No, I want to bawl my fucking eyes out. As I sit in this SUV being driven by one of Alessandro De Luca's men with him beside me, I want to break down and fall apart because I realize whole-heartedly I could lose the two most important people in my life today.

The goal is for Declan and his men to save Scarlet and come home safe and sound, but I'm not so naïve not to know an operation like this could go terribly wrong.

Alessandro pats the back of my hand, making me startle.

"He's going to be okay, bella. Declan is one of the smartest men I've ever known. He will make sure to come home to you. Just believe in him."

I nod at the handsome Italian man. He's around Declan's age, tall and muscular, but where Declan's eyes are green, his are a deep shade of gray. Even though I'm not blind and can see he's definitely a catch, I feel absolutely no attraction toward him because I only have eyes for one man, and that man is risking his life for my happiness.

"I do believe in him. I'm just so scared. My sister is my

best friend, and if I lost both of them…" I trail off because a sob catches in my throat and I can't get anything else out.

He gives me a soft smile and squeezes my hand. "I know, bella. I know what it's like to lose someone you love. That's not going to happen with you."

I can tell by his words he's been through some shit that has scarred him, but before I can ask any questions, I hear several loud pops. Glass explodes into the SUV. We're pushed sideways as more pops ring through the air.

"Fuck!" Alessandro shouts.

Suddenly there are men everywhere outside of the vehicles, guns in their hands as they fire back and forth at each other.

"Get out of the car, bella. We need to get to the car ahead," Alessandro shouts. "I'm right behind you. The doors are reinforced so stay down."

I'm in so much shock I can't move. My entire body starts to shake.

"Bella, go!" he shouts, pushing me toward the door.

He reaches over me, opens the door, and practically shoves me out, then pulls me down low as he leads me to the first car in line.

Everything feels like it's going in slow motion. We take step after step, the gunfire so loud, and bullets flying. We're on a mostly deserted country road. No other cars other than the SUVs.

Just as we're getting to the first car, Ivan rounds the hood. His spine-chilling gaze lands on me. Alessandro pulls a gun, but before he can shoot, Ivan fires three times. I scream as Alessandro crumples to the ground. I start to try to help him, but I'm yanked by my hair, and Ivan drags me away.

Within seconds, I'm in another SUV. The wheels screech as it takes off with Ivan sitting across from me, pointing a gun at my head.

"Your man thought he was going to get one over on me.

He thought he would send you away so I couldn't get to you, but he's not as smart as he thinks he is. I've been watching him. I knew your sister wouldn't mean enough to him to actually give up his territory. But for his wife... he'll give up everything."

I'm shaking like a leaf as I process his words. "He won't give it up," I murmur.

Searing pain hits my cheek as he backhands me with the gun still in his grip. My entire face burns, and tears well in my eyes, but I will not let this man see me cry. He's a coward. Only a coward would do the shit he's done. I won't let him see my fear or pain. I won't. I've met guys like this before. All my life, men like him were dragged in and out of our lives by my mother, and they get off on causing women pain. I won't give him the fucking satisfaction.

My only hope is that he's taking me to the same place as Scarlet. I need to see her. I need to know she's alive and okay. I'll put my life on the line for her and Declan. I just need her to be okay.

He's breathing heavily, and when he grabbed me, I noticed his blown pupils. The guy is on something, and I pray that whatever it is, it makes his heart explode.

"Where's Scarlet?" I ask.

He lets out an evil laugh that makes a chill run through me. "That bitch is right where she needs to be. Fucking whore."

I see red as he talks about my sister like that, but I need to keep it together. I want to punch him, but the guy driving the SUV would probably shoot me on the spot if I did anything to his boss.

There is absolutely nothing I can do. I'm pretty sure I'm dead. I just pray Declan can at least get my sister out of there.

The pink diamond on my ring finger catches my attention as it sparkles in the sunlight coming through the tinted windows. I have to bite my lip to keep myself from crying as I think of the last however many months it's been since I met the big, bad wolf at Surrender. All the good things that have happened in my life that I now know my Daddy is responsible for. I may have only called him my Daddy for a few days, but he's been that to me much longer than I ever knew. I'll never know what made me so special in his eyes, but I'm so grateful I had the chance to experience love and romance before I die. I hope he understands how much I truly do love him.

30

DECLAN

"Declan! Her tracker stopped suddenly and is now going in the wrong direction," Grady says over the phone.

Every cell in my body tenses. "Fuck!" I roar. "Where?"

"She's headed to the Petrov estate."

"Go! Fucking faster!" I shout at Connor.

He pushes down on the gas, and we're racing toward Vladimir's compound as Killian's phone starts ringing.

"Yeah?" he barks as he puts it on speaker.

"The boss has been shot. We were fucking ambushed. Ivan took her," a man with an Italian accent says.

I can't control my rage as I start punching the seat in front of me. Fuck! How did this happen? How could I *let* this happen? How could I have possibly thought she'd be safer with someone else?

Connor is driving well over a hundred miles an hour. The other cars match his speed.

"We go in the same way we planned. From all different directions. How close is she?" I shout.

"They look to be about a mile from the estate," Grady says.

We're only about three but at the pace we're going, we may get there at the same time. I'm going to rip his fucking head off with my bare hands. How dare he even *think* of touching my girl. I was just going to shoot and kill him, nice and clean. Not now. I'm going to torture him and cause him endless amounts of pain before I let him die.

I look at Killian. "You go after Scarlet and get her the fuck out of there."

He doesn't respond other than a nod. He's too angry and right now, we're both ready to kill.

"We're approaching the estate," Connor says.

Killian and I draw our guns. The SUV in front of us will drive through the gates, firing. I hope to God this fucking bastard hasn't already hurt my baby girl.

"They just passed the gates," Grady calls out.

Fucking good.

The next few minutes happen so quickly they feel like only seconds. We're through the gate. Bullets fly from every direction. Ivan's SUV speeds away, deeper into the property. Connor stops just long enough for Killian to jump out of the car before he guns it to follow Ivan. A few of my guys follow Killian, but most stay with me. I came here to save Scarlet, but saving my Little girl is now my top priority.

We're deep into the property in a fielded area when Ivan's SUV comes to a stop. Connor slams on the brakes, and I'm out of the car in seconds with Grady, Bash, Ronan, and several dozen soldiers right there with me.

Ivan pulls Cali out of his car by her hair, and it takes everything inside of me not to rush him. He has a gun to her head, and I'm under no delusion this man isn't crazy enough to shoot her. As soon as she sees me, she tries to break free, but he yanks her back. She cries out in pain. Her cheek is an angry purple. Blood trickles down the side. I've never felt so scared in my entire life.

My men know not to make a move until I signal, but I

can see my brothers struggling not to shoot Ivan. It's too risky, though. He has Cali so fucking close to him. Even with Ronan being the best shooter of the bunch, he could still miss and hit her by accident.

"What do you want, Ivan? You name it, and it's yours," I offer.

Over my fucking dead body will this bastard get anything. No matter what, he's a dead man. He's stupid not to realize that no matter what happens, he's going down along with the entire organization his father worked so hard to build. If I were a better man, I'd only take out Ivan, but I'm not. Not even close.

His hand shakes as he holds the gun to her temple. She winces and sucks in a breath, and I silently tell her to hold on for just a few more seconds.

Out of the corner of my eye, I see Ronan give a slight tug to his suit jacket. Cali's gaze darts to him. He's signaling something to her. It takes me a second to put it together. She shifts slightly, backing closer to Ivan so her back is pressed against his front. She's trying to figure out if he has another gun under his jacket. She feels it, and a smile flashes briefly. My tough girl.

Ivan is so fucking high he didn't catch the silent conversation between my brother and my wife. He's sweating profusely, and his eyes are darting everywhere.

"I want everything. All the territory," Ivan yells.

This guy is a fucking moron. I swear to God he doesn't have a brain cell in his head.

"You have to let her go," I say.

He shakes his head. "Not until I have the paperwork. Tell your men to put their guns down!"

I move my gaze to Cali and raise my eyebrow just slightly. She nods.

"Okay. Okay. But you let her go once we do."

Ivan snorts and pushes the gun against her temple even

harder. I'm blinded with pure fucking rage. I just need to keep it in check for a few seconds longer.

"Put your guns down!" I order.

They know me. They know based on my wording that until I give a second command, they aren't to lower their weapons. Most of these men have trained their entire lives for moments like this, and they know exactly what to do.

I lock eyes with my girl then lower them to Ivan's feet before I look back up at her. She shifts in his hold slightly, but Ivan is too distracted to notice her subtle movements.

I make the command again. "Put your guns down. Now!"

My men start lowering their guns to the ground. Ivan watches them while Cali darts her hand inside his suit jacket and grabs his gun. As soon as it's free from the holster, she points it at his foot and fires.

He screams in pain and his arm loosens enough for her to drop to the ground. As soon as she does, I put a full magazine of bullets through him. I won't get to torture him before he dies, but at this point, I just want him dead so I can get to my girl.

I scoop her up, running to the armored SUV while the rest of my guys surround Ivan and start shooting at his approaching men.

As soon as we're in the vehicle, Connor speeds away from the scene. I hold my sobbing girl against my chest so tight I hardly think either of us can breathe. I don't need oxygen, though. She's the only thing I need.

"Daddy," she cries.

"I'm here, baby. Fuck, I'm so sorry. I'm so sorry, Cali."

Sobs rack her body as she clings to me. I have no idea where Killian is or what Scarlet's status is, but right now my only concern in Cali.

Connor's phone rings, and when he answers it, I can hear Killian shouting before the call ends.

"He has Scarlet and is on his way to the house," Connor tells us.

Cali's sobbing becomes hysterical. She's starting to hyperventilate, so I pull her away from my chest and grab her chin roughly so she's forced to look at me.

"Cali, breathe. In and out. Slow. Breathe, baby. Shh."

She tries to follow my instructions, but it takes several minutes before she's almost breathing normally. Her tears are still falling, and she's trembling so hard it's starting to worry me.

I hold her on my lap as Connor makes his way through the city. My men will tell me if Ivan is dead or alive later. I really fucking hope he's alive because I want to make him pay dearly for this wound on my baby girl's face.

"Daddy's got you. Shh," I murmur as I rock her against me.

While we were able to get Cali and Scarlet, I have no doubt the war will go on for days to come until we get complete control of the Russians. My guess is that most of them will be thrilled Ivan's no longer their boss, but there are probably a few of his faithful followers that will want revenge. That's fine. They can come. Cali isn't leaving my fucking sight for the rest of our lives. She thought I was overprotective before. That will be laughable compared to how it will be going forward.

"Alessandro," she whimpers. "Is he okay?"

I stare down at her worried face, unable to answer because I have no clue who's dead or alive. Quite frankly, I don't really care at the moment. She's safe in my arms.

31

CALI

My body is numb as he rocks me. I can't comprehend everything that's happened in the last couple of hours. I don't think I even want to try. The only thing I want is to go home with my Daddy and see my sister. I want to make sure she's okay, and I'm afraid of what I might see when we finally get to her.

It feels like forever before Connor pulls up to Declan's house. I try to scramble free so I can jump out of the car and find my sister, but Declan's arms tighten around me, and he shakes his head. Fear etches his face, and I realize he *needs* to hold me right now.

I snuggle into him and wait for him to carry me into the house. As soon as we get inside, one of the guards tells Declan where Killian went with Scarlet.

Declan takes me down an unfamiliar hallway. When he stops and opens the door, I see a sterile room—almost like a hospital room—where Scarlet clings to Killian as he holds her like a baby in his arms.

"Scar!" I cry out.

I struggle, and Declan sets me on my feet. I run to her, horrified by the sight in front of me. She's filthy and bruised

229

all over. Her skin is almost a shade of gray. She's lost a lot of weight, and her eyes are sunk into her face, but as soon as she sees me, she releases her arms from around Killian's neck and reaches for me as I crash into her.

"Cali!" she sobs. "I'm so sorry. I'm so fucking sorry."

We cling to each other until there's a knock at the door and a man in a white coat walks in.

"Baby, we need the doctor to examine you and Scarlet," Declan says from behind me, his fingers stroking my back.

Reluctantly, I release my sister as tears continue to stream down my cheeks. I look back at Declan and shake my head. "I'm fine. I don't need to be looked at."

Declan raises his eyebrow, lifts me from the foot of the bed, and pulls me against his chest. "Daddy decides, and you're going to get checked over, but I'll let the doctor check your sister out first."

A shiver runs through me because even though I don't like doctors, I need my Daddy's control more than anything right now. "'Kay, Daddy," I whisper against his neck.

"I'm going to take her up and give her a bath, Doc. When you're done with Scarlet, come to my room," Declan commands as he heads toward the door.

The thought of leaving my sister makes me panic, and I start clawing at his suit.

As if he understands, Declan pauses his stride, then pivots and carries me back to Scarlet. "Give her one more hug. As soon as you two are checked over and clean, you can spend as much time as you want with her, but right now, you both need care."

With a whimper, I reach down and hug Scarlet for a long moment. When we release each other, our eyes stay locked together as I'm carried from the room.

Declan holds me close as he makes his way up the stairs. "She's going to be okay, baby girl. I'll make sure of it."

I nod and nestle my face against his neck, taking in his

scent. I'm home. Right where I'm supposed to be, and my family is safe.

———————

DECLAN HASN'T STOPPED HOVERING since he brought me upstairs. I hate his tormented expression. He's angry with himself, and he needs to stop because none of this is his fault. But even though I've only known him for a short time, I know he's the type of man that takes the blame when things go wrong.

"Daddy."

He looks down at me as I sit in a bubble bath. He already cleaned the wound on my face, though my cheek feels like it has its own heartbeat. Not that I'll tell him that and make him worry more than he already is.

I reach up with a wet hand and touch his cheek. "I'm okay."

The sound he makes tells me he doesn't believe me. "He could have killed you, Cali."

"Yes, he could have, but he didn't. Because you and the rest of your men came and saved me. Because your brother taught me how to use a gun. I'm safe. It's over."

His green eyes burn into me as he leans into my touch. "I could have lost you."

I nod. "Yeah, but you didn't. We're both here and tormenting yourself over it isn't going to help."

"You're never leaving my sight again," he murmurs.

A smile pulls at my lips. "Good. It was a stupid idea to send me away anyway."

My smart comment causes his lips to twitch, and some of the fire I love seeing in his eyes returns.

"It was a stupid idea. Next time I'm locking you in my dungeon where no one can ever find you."

That makes me giggle. "Ohhh, are there chains down there too? It could be like a kinky role-play type of thing."

He bursts out laughing and shakes his head. "Stop making jokes, brat. I'm being fucking serious."

"Yeah, about that. You need to stop being so serious."

A smile tugs at his lips as he leans down and brushes his mouth against mine. "I love you, Cali Ann Gilroy. Don't ever fucking scare me like that again, okay? I've never been so frightened in my entire life."

I reach up and wrap my arms around his neck, soaking the collar of his suit, but neither of us care. "I love you, too, Daddy."

When he pulls his mouth away and stares down at me, I can tell he's still upset but maybe a smidge less. I'll take what I can get. It's going to take time for him to get over this. It's going to take me time too. Hell, I shot a man today. Although it felt really freaking good when I pulled the trigger and made him howl like the little punk he is.

Declan takes his time as he pulls me from the tub and dries me with several fluffy towels before he drops one of his oversized white T-shirts over my head and puts me into bed.

"You're not leaving this bed for at least a week, Little girl."

I let out a noise of protest. "Yes, huh. I need to see Scarlet."

He wants to argue with me, but doesn't. He knows how much Scarlet means to me, and even though he would keep me in bed for a week or more if he could, I know he'll never keep me away from her.

"Fine, I'll put you both in bed together, and neither of you are leaving it for two weeks," he growls.

I can't stop myself from giggling. "How did it just go from one week to two weeks, and why am I getting grounded because of that fuckhead?"

His lips twitch again. "No cursing. Just because you're

hurt doesn't mean I won't figure out a punishment for saying naughty words."

God, this man is as stubborn as a donkey, but I swear, I think I fall more and more in love with him with each bossy thing he says.

"Fine, why am I grounded for what that fudgehead did?"

Before he can respond, the French doors burst open, and a wild-eyed Bash, along with Ronan, Grady, and Keiran storm in. I startle and make a yelping noise that has Declan practically foaming at the mouth as he growls at them.

"Lass! Fuck, you're okay," Bash says, completely ignoring Declan as he comes to my bedside.

I nod and smile as he takes my hand in his, kissing the back of it. "I'm good, Bash. Are you guys okay?"

They all nod, and Grady steps forward, brushing his hand over my hair. "We're good, lass. You gave us a scare, though. You're not leaving our sight ever again."

Fudge. It's not just Declan who's going to be even more overprotective from now on. I have a feeling I won't be able to tinkle on my own without one of them in the room. Hmm, I don't really hate that either. I feel part of something for once in my life. A real family. I just hope they'll accept Scarlet like they have me.

My eyes catch Ronan who's standing a few feet away from the bed observing me in silence. When our gazes meet, he smiles and winks. "You did good, Little one. Really fucking good."

I break out into a wide grin at his praise. "Thanks, snitch."

Ronan chuckles and rolls his eyes.

"Has anyone heard anything about Alessandro?"

Keiran nods. "He's fine. Two gunshot wounds to his shoulder, but his vest caught the others. He's being patched up by his doctor and said he'll stop by as soon as he's done."

Relief floods me. "And Ivan?"

Declan looks to his men, and I see some sort of silent communication between them before Grady smiles at me. "He's dead, lass. No more worrying about him."

For the first time since my sister met that loser, I feel an invisible weight lift from me.

The doctor who was downstairs taps on the open door before he steps in with a smile. I sit straight up. "How's Scarlet?"

"She's good. Stable. Getting some IV fluids as we speak. Her Daddy is down there holding her while she sleeps. She'll probably sleep a lot over the next few days."

I furrow my brows. "She doesn't have a Daddy."

The older man returns my confused look with one of his own. "Huh. He didn't correct me when I called her his Little girl."

Something inside of me flutters, and I look at Declan. He seems to be having some sort of epiphany. His lips twitch at the corners. When I give him a quizzical look, he just gives a slight shake of his head.

The doctor shrugs and steps toward the bed. "Let's get you checked out, Little one, shall we?"

32

DECLAN

I stand in front of the bastard who hurt my Little girl
and smile as blood drips from his face. Like my guys,
he'd been wearing a bulletproof vest, so my shots took
him down to the ground but didn't kill him. My men secured
him and brought him to one of my warehouses where the few
bullet wounds to his arms have continued to bleed since last
night while he's been chained to a wall. Fitting, as that's what
he did to Scarlet. No food, no bathroom, and no heat. By the
time I walked in three hours ago, he was begging for death.

I've been taking my time torturing him. Killian, Grady,
Ronan, and Keiran are all here. I left Bash with the girls —
along with a dozen more guards — while we handle this. I
trust my men completely, but these six are the ones I trust
the most. They'll do anything in their power to protect Cali
and Scarlet, so one of us will always be with them.

Killian has been taking turns with me on Ivan, and I'm
quickly realizing this is as personal to my best friend as it is
me. I can see by the way he looks at Scarlet that even though
she doesn't know it yet, he's claimed her. Maybe I'm just
imagining shit, but I've never seen my friend look at any
Little like that in all our years. And even though he really

doesn't know Scarlet, I can't say shit because it only took one look at Cali to know she was mine.

Two hours later, the five of us leave the warehouse while several of my men work to clean up the blood and remains of Ivan Petrov. I'm prepared for war with the Russians, but so far it seems the new leader stepping into Ivan's role just wants to work things out civilly, which is fine with me. We'll see. Either way, I'm ready to protect what's mine.

WHEN WE ARRIVE BACK at the house, I'm about to head upstairs to the guest room where the girls have been resting together when I hear giggling from deeper on the first level of the house. We follow the sound and turn the corner into the living room to find Cali and Bash on the couch watching a movie, Bash sitting on the couch while Cali is on the floor with her legs crossed and a blanket over her lap. She has Snickers clutched in one of her hands. She looks fucking adorable. But even adorable girls still get in trouble when they disobey their Daddies.

I clear my throat, making Cali startle and turn to me, wide-eyed with a deer in the headlights look. Her bruised cheek is a deep shade of angry purple that makes me want to go back to that warehouse and kill Ivan all over again.

"Hi, Daddy!" she says sweetly.

I'm thrilled she just called me Daddy in front of my guys, but she knows she's busted. The doctor gave Scarlet some pretty intense painkillers to deal with the bruising Ivan caused when he'd first kidnapped her, so she's been sleeping most of the time. Cali hadn't wanted to leave her sister, so I'd made her a deal. As long as she stayed in the bed, she could stay with Scarlet. My Little girl knows she's busted.

I put my hands on my hips and raise an eyebrow. "What are you doing out of bed, Little miss?"

Her eyes dart to Bash, who holds his hands up. "I told you. Don't look to me for protection. You're on your own, lass."

She looks up at me and then at the guys standing behind me. Killian has disappeared, and my first guess is that he's gone up to check on Scarlet.

"I'm resting, Daddy. See, I have a blanket and Snickers, and we're watching a movie. It's the same as being in bed and doing it, but I'm down here," she rushes to say.

This sweet Little naughty girl is killing me. It's only a matter of time before she's walking all over me. Hell, she probably already is.

"Whether you're resting down here or not, your rule was to stay in bed," I reply.

Her shoulders drop, and then she does something I'm not expecting. She throws herself back onto the floor and kicks her feet with a pout on her lips. Bash and Keiran snicker quietly while Ronan lets out a low whistle and Grady clears his throat in a clear attempt to keep himself from laughing.

I give her an incredulous look. "Cali Ann Gilroy, are you having a tantrum?"

She's still on her back looking up at me when she nods. "I'm tired of being in bed. It's so boring. Scarlet's too sleepy to talk to me. Bashie said we could watch a movie."

I narrow my eyes at my brother, who glares down at Cali.

"Cali Ann, I said I would sit up in the room with you and watch a movie. You're the one who came down here and started one while I was getting you a snack," Bash scolds.

To my shock and utter amusement, Cali sticks her tongue out at Bash. "Snitches get stitches, Bashie. Is that what you want? Stitches?"

My brother's eyes widen as he stares down at her, and I can't even hold back a soft chuckle.

"She's a fucking savage," he mumbles.

"You," I say pointing to her, "get up and let's go upstairs."

The only response I get from her is another kick of her feet. Without hesitating, I pluck her up from the floor, but instead of wrapping herself around me like a baby koala, she goes deadweight in my arms. Her theatrics make me grin as I shift and throw her over my shoulder, giving her bottom a sharp smack that has her yelping.

My guys grin as I walk out of the room with her, and as I start making my way up the stairs, I feel her fingers brush over my ass before she pinches it. I give her several sharp smacks on her cheeks in return, making her giggle.

"You're such a naughty girl, Cali. What am I going to do with you?"

She giggles again. "Love me forever and ever?"

I grin as we enter our bedroom. "Oh, I'm going to love you forever and ever, but you're still getting your ass spanked, and then you're getting tucked back into bed."

All I get in return is a huff from her, but when I lower her onto her feet, she's smiling up at me.

I take her face in my hands and press a kiss to her lips. "I just want what's best for you."

With a sigh, she nods. "I know, Daddy. Will you hang out with me in bed at least?"

"Of course. Let's get your spanking over with, and then I'll snuggle you all day."

She nods and wraps her arms around my waist. "I love you, Daddy."

My heart swells in my chest as I wrap my arms around her and press a kiss to the top of her head. "I love you, too, baby. Forever and ever."

Are you ready to read Killian and Scarlet's story? Click Here or scan the QR code below!

Interested in reading more Daddies who will do anything to protect their women?

CHECK out my Daddies of the Shadows series by clicking here or scanning the QR code below. These Daddies are hot, possessive, dangerous, and will stop at nothing to protect the ones they love.

KEEP UP WITH KATE!

Sign up for my newsletter get teasers, cover reveals, updates, and extra content!

SCAN ME TO SIGN UP NOW!

ALSO BY KATE OLIVER

West Coast Daddies Series

Ally's Christmas Daddy

Haylee's Hero Daddy

Maddie's Daddy Crush

Safe With Daddy

Trusting Her Daddy

Ruby's Forever Daddies

Daddies of the Shadows Series

Knox

Ash

Beau

Wolf

Leo

Maddox

Colt

Hawk

Angel

Tate

Rawhide Ranch

A Little Fourth of July Fiasco

Shadowridge Guardians

(A multi-author series)

Kade

Syndicate Kings

Corrupting Cali: Declan's Story

Daddies of Pine Hollow

Jaxon

PLEASE LEAVE A REVIEW!

It would mean so much to me if you would take a brief moment to leave a rating and/or a review on this book. It helps other readers find me. Thank you for your support!

-Kate

Made in the USA
Columbia, SC
10 October 2023

24244755R00137